RE: INCARNATION

Susan Webb

ISBN:-13: 978-0615761886 (World TriadPublishing)
ISBN-10: 0615761887

To my husband, Doug Webb.
Thank you for your patience.

Chapter 1

It was ethereal in its physical description but not with the pious emotion that overlaps the term. The subtle lighting iridescently diffused the whiteness of room. The air was cooler than the water so a misty white cloud clung to the surface like an inverted sky. It smelled of chlorine.

Amelia popped up from her final lap in the pool, breathless and fatigued. The diving board sprung and she turned to watch a diver pierce the water, leaving barely a splash. She waited for him to surface then watched him pull his distinct and dripping body from the pool to climb the ladder again. She couldn't stop staring and was suddenly embarrassed by her actions. Shaking her head to clear the image she pulled herself from the pool, walked to the bench and grabbed her towel. From behind she heard her coach, "Great effort today kiddo. That last fifty was your best time. Try to tuck your head earlier in the turns." Amelia peeled off her red Speedo swim cap so she could better hear and damp blonde hair tumbled to her shoulders. Her coach turned, not waiting for a response, and walked away. She was headed for the locker room when again she heard the spring and the wobble of the diving board.

Previous budget shortfalls had cost Iowa State University both its baseball team and its men's swimming and diving program. As promised by the new forward thinking Athletic Director, men's swimming and diving was now back on the roster as a locally pioneering collaboration, consolidating the men's and women's practice facility at Byer pool.

The budding star of the University's dive team was freshman Alex William Garreth, possibly the Darwinian link between man, bird and fish. He honed his well chiseled form with a strict and determined regiment; weight training every morning followed by a half hour free style frenzy in the pool. All of this he accomplished before an 8 AM ethics class. It was what he liked to do in his spare time. Co-ed, organized team practice followed in the afternoon.

Alex flew like an osprey when he left the board. His arms stretched up to a perfect point, his toes together and sharp like he was threading the eye of a needle with his body then gracefully bending, spiking and twirling just inches from the end of the still wobbling board before being swallowed by a pool that seemed to open with a space made only for his perfectly formed body leaving behind him scarcely a splash to say he had once been there. He popped up from the water at the pool's edge to the uproarious cheers of his teammates. Although used to the attention, it still left him slightly embarrassed. He smiled a sincere, humble smile and pulled his dripping, sculpted body from the pool.

"I can offer no words to improve that dive… excellent," the dive coach exclaimed. "But…*please*, for your safety try to put an inch of space between your head and the board."

Alex smiled wryly. It was precisely the feedback he'd wanted. Coach tossed him a towel and walked away eliminating the obstacle behind which Amelia had hid. Now she found her eyes fixed on his. He neither smiled nor frowned; he didn't react at all, but his gaze made her uncomfortable. She brought her towel up to wipe her face and walked into the dressing room.

It was after 3PM when she left the pool. Her hair, still wet, hung from a pony tail pulled through the back of a tan ball cap. With a book bag on one shoulder she waited at the bus stop for the bus to arrive. After a short time she stepped onto the Cy ride; appropriately named for the ISU Cyclone's mascot, it was occupied mostly by college students. She took a seat and waited for the bus to jerk away but instead the doors hissed open again and Alex got on. "Thanks for holding it for me Doris" he said fondly to the toothy, grinning bus driver; a portly, middle aged woman with short, frizzy, burnt orange hair – a home dye job gone bad. Her odor, Amelia had noticed, was cheap cigarettes and even cheaper perfume.

"Oh sure, always looking out for *you* don't ya know," said Doris with a heavy Nordic drawl.

Alex sat in a seat within earshot of Doris. He leaned forward and put his hands on his knees; appearing earnestly engaged in conversation.

Amelia thought to herself sarcastically, "Do all woman fawn over him? How can he live with himself? What an ego." She stared loathingly yet unintentionally memorizing the way his wavy black hair looped carelessly into perfect loose curls. She had a side view of his strong features and saw his eyes smile as he laughed at something Doris had said. Although Amelia wanted to be repulsed, his laughter was infectious and made her smile.

Her stop was approaching. She pulled the cord to sound the bell. When the bus slowed, she walked down the narrow aisle to the exit. The bus lurched when it came to a full stop and Amelia almost fell into Alex's lap. He put his hands on her waist to steady her. When she regained her balance he bent without standing and recovered a book that had fallen. "Here you go" is all he said when he handed it back to her. She felt her face flush with embarrassment as she looked again into his eyes. She took the book and leapt from the bus without a word.

The bus rolled away from the stop and Alex looked back over his shoulder watching Amelia shrink into the fading midday sun. "Sure enough is a cutie that girl there," said Doris. Alex said nothing but watched her disappear. The bus came to a stop in front of a low rent trailer park. Alex stood to exit, as the door opened Doris said, "You really should get yourself a girl ya know and I think ya got one in mind – just talk to her why don't ya?" Alex smiled mischievously and said, "What do I need another girl in my life for? I'd feel like I was cheating on you. I'll see ya Monday – you be good and be careful out there." He winked and stepped from the bus.

As Alex walked past the rows of older deteriorating trailer homes, a dog began to bark and jump at the chain linked fence. The brown short-haired mutt had a shrill bark for a dog of his great bulk. Alex stopped at the fence and set his back pack down. He pulled out half a bologna sandwich wrapped in ziplock bag. The dog became more excited and bounced hard against the fence. Alex flipped the sandwich in the air over the fence and the Pit mix soared through the air catching and swallowing it before hitting the ground. The effort to swallow the sandwich whole silenced him for a moment.

"Damn – Bruiser chew that thing first. You're gonna choke to death."

The dog hacked up the sandwich and scarfed the remains down again, this time chewing the chunks. Alex leaned over the fence and scratched Bruiser behind the ear then crossed the street to his own single wide.

The living area was sparsely furnished… a tattered sofa; plaid with stuffing peeking out from well-worn arms and a small TV that sat atop a piece of press board which straddled two cinder blocks. There were Nike posters and Gatorade posters featuring pictures of divers in motion. Alex opened the coat closet. On the floor was a large cardboard box filled with trophies and medals. He tossed his gym bag on top of the box and closed the door.

***

A door opened and Amelia stepped out of her apartment; she carried a small overnight bag. After locking her apartment door, she bounded down the steps. Highway 30 was already a speedway. Four wheel drive monsters and muddy farm trucks paraded past her in the fast lane. They dwarfed her in the sun-faded, 1978 once red Chevette. The car had been her mother's first and only new car and was handed down to Amelia when she was seventeen as transportation to and from swim meets and later to college. Her mother rarely drove; she was almost always with her husband if she was away from the farm, so the car had remarkably low miles for a ten year old vehicle.

There was too much traffic for Amelia's comfort so she decided to take the back roads. It added twenty minutes to her drive but the scenic route was more to her liking today. It was a beautiful autumn afternoon.

The Midwest sky is like no other at harvest time. Particles of grain dust become trapped in the air. Sunlight doesn't penetrate the grain dust – it reflects off of it creating dusk and dawn hews that are unique to time and place.

And the aroma! Grain dust has a sort of pungent, herbaceous smell with both texture and taste. The decomposing leaves and grass have an earthy mildewed quality. The combination creates an intoxicating bouquet.

Amelia drove with her car window down to absorb all of the senses of fall. She traveled along the narrow gravel road to a four way stop where she paused to turned off her car radio before driving on. Nearby a whippoorwill signaled the coming evening. A red winged blackbird clung sideways to a cattail which stood tall with others in a steep ditch beside her car. Climbing the far side of the ditch, a stand of sumac blazed their autumn best. All of the familiar images, flavors and melodies she savored with harmonizing nostalgia.

When Amelia rounded the curve just past her four-way, she dropped her visor to shield her eyes from the glare of the setting sun. There are a few minutes in every autumn evening when the sun reaches a point in the sky so that the rays are brilliantly magnified by grain dust. It's blindingly bright and nearly impossible to look in the direction of the sun. Amelia averted her eyes and looked to the road side so she could judge the path of the road.

The extended arm of the International Harvester peeled back the top of the faded Chevette like a pop top tuna can.

Chapter 2

The uppercut landed squarely beneath his chin, lifting Evron Brown from his feet and depositing him onto the hard concrete. A crowd of thirty or more followers had gathered to witness the championship brawl for the title in Des Moines' underworld of street fighting. Blood streamed from the grotesque ruptured orb of flesh which was the engorged remnant of his right eye lid. Each breath was an acute stabbing reminder of the multiple blows to the ribs he had taken early in the fight. He wanted to stay down, to let the cool pavement sooth the pain, but the nipping mongrel of defeat drove him to his feet again as a swell of encouragement grew within the crowd for the fallen champ; it was a low and melodic mantra; King Brown, King Brown, King Brown.

In the twelve years that Evron had been a competitive street fighter his record was 47-4. He had recently gone three years

10

undefeated. Now, at forty-two, he would lose again. When his head hit the pavement the thud was like a ripe melon striking the ground. The crowd was instantly silent. In the distance police sirens wailed and most of the crowd scattered. Some, however, left hesitantly; waiting and hoping to see Evron stand again. Even his opponent hesitated – standing over the crumpled body of his challenger – a pool of blood streamed from the back of Evron's head and gathered around Dirk's boots. With a look of horror and panic, Dirk Cooper stepped hastily over the body. He kicked his Kawasaki Ninja into high gear and screamed down the alley turning the corner just as the first patrol car arrived.

"This is Delta 19 – we've got a man unconscious and badly beaten, looks like head trauma with severe blood loss. Request paramedics to west lot of IBP packing plant at 1800 Maury St." Two officers stood in the silent and deserted lot of the packing plant where minutes before an uproarious crowd cheered. No trace remained of the event, but the defeated and fallen ex-champion, Evron James Brown.

When Dirk was certain he hadn't been seen by the police, he slowed his speed and turned into a residential neighborhood. He could feel his heartbeat reverberate in his sternum sending coordinating throbs into his throat. His lungs were in a state of spasm that made it seem as if he was trying to breathe through a pixie straw. Dirk was beaten and bloody – his shirt damp with his blood and Evron's. Adrenalin fed his body with a mixture of personal fear and private horror. Had he just killed a man, he wondered. The sight of the big black man's head striking the pavement haunted him and he recalled every second and every sound of the final blow in an exaggerated frame of time. A car behind him honked and he realized that he'd come to a stop in the middle of the dark street. He kicked up the bike and sped through the trailing edge of the residential street that led to a two-lane and into farm country. The motor staggered a growl as Dirk shifted rapidly through the gears.

He was near top speed when he blew past the patrol car that lay in wait on old Bondurant Road. Hugging his bike, looking only at the road, he was unaware of the patrol car. The patrol radioed for assistance and Dirk heard the sirens from the second vehicle as it pulled nearly in front of him. He looked over his shoulder at the two distant sets of spinning lights. He knew they couldn't catch him but they would keep calling in reinforcements ahead to stop him. Bondurant, a small farming town, was about six miles away – a stoplight, two bars, a co-op and a post office. It was a straight shot into town, however, the road ahead was fortified by a set of paralleling railroad tracks separated a few yards apart by a violent dip in the road that would send him air born at his current speed. Before taking on the tracks he slowed and cut the lights. When he entered town he killed the engine and glided and around back of the co-op. He reached in his pocket and drew out a cigarette. Sirens now rapidly approached. From where Dirk sat he could see the first car take flight. When it landed the undercarriage struck and scraped the concrete creating a spectacular show of sparks. The second car followed just moments behind; his breaks screeched and rubber smoked the air as he tried to keep from catching and crushing the lead car. The squeal and the screaming sirens caught the sleepy town's attention and like ants to a sweet morsel, the residents rushed into the street as the squad cars shrieked out of sight. Dirk lit and finished another cigarette… while the residents crept back into their daily lives. When all was calm, he pushed his bike out from the back of the co-op and behind the privacy fence of the Dew Drop Inn.

***

"Jesus!" Mart said "You missed all of the excitement Dirk." In a town where Betty Jo; a single mom who gave birth to twins of mixed ethnicity, had been the current topic of chatter, a police chase was an exciting diversion. Earl slapped his dusty Levis with his Garst seed corn cap and exclaimed. "They damn near run me over; I had to hustle to get out the way. Yes sir they must been goin' hundred, hundred n' ten wouldn't ya say Bernie?" he said to his unresponsive friend of equal attire and age – ancient and dirty. Earl continued, "They must a been chasin' a damn murderer or something the way they was

13

movin'." Earl continued to talk making gestures with his hands about how the cars got airborne while the patrons of the bar listened and nodded as if agreeing with the animated storyteller. Although Earl, Bernie and Dirk were the town's only witnesses, Earl's recount would be claimed as fact by most of the bar's occupants as the story would evolve.

Mart looked at Dirk and his face went pallid with recognition of the situation. He pulled a Dew Drop Inn tee shirt off the hanger where it hung for sale behind the bar and tossed it to Dirk. When Dirk looked down at his faded yellow T-shirt he noticed the Harley Davidson logo was barely recognizable through the soaking of dried blood and sweat. He turned and walked to the bath room at the back of the bar; washed his face, his pits and his chest with wadded handfuls of paper towels and threw his shirt in the waste basket. When he emerged from the bathroom, Mart, the bartender and owner, noticed the swelling over Dirk's left eye. It was turning jaundice purple and his knuckles were red, swollen and cut. Mart had a Jack and Coke waiting for him. "Did you win or lose?" asked Mart trying to judge from the beating he had apparently taken. "I didn't lose." said Dirk. He smoked another cigarette, drank the Jack and Coke and sat quietly for what seemed to him a condensed eternity.

Chapter 3

Florescent ceiling lights rolled past like the box cars on a freight train while bits and pieces of transient conversations raced by. A surgical masked face leaned over her. The voices became briefly discernible. "Dear God, what happened to this poor girl? We might be able to save her life but she's not winning any beauty pageant."

The masked face blurred. The room spun faster and faster. As the spinning slowed, white fluffy clouds against a beautiful blue sky came into focus. A little girl in denim overalls and a white and floral print tee shirt held on to a homemade tree swing's fraying ropes. Her head was tossed back so that her nose pointed skyward. When the swing lost its forward momentum it began a brief counter rotation then rocked on a pendulum until it finally stopped. The little girl, eyes closed, hung motionless until a fat, brown, shaggy dog waddled happily up to lick her forehead. The little girl let go of the rope and

slid backward off the seat of the swing giggling while the dog
continued to lick. She lay on her back with her hands over her face.
The dog circled her then lay down almost on top of her and rested its
big head on its furry paws.

"Millie, go tell your father its dinner time." She heard her
mother say. The screen door bounced shut. She lay on the ground for
a moment curling her fingers in the old dog's coat with one hand the
other was hooked under the back of her head. She watched the fluffy
clouds drift by. All at once Millie sprang to her feet and raced off.
After just a few feet she turned and patted her leg for the dog to
follow. "Let's go Cookie," she said. Her hand me-down Huffy lay on
its side near a flower bed that was losing its summer colors. Most of
the poppies had gone to seed, their skeletons rattled in the breeze.
Next to her bike was a tennis ball. She picked up the yellow ball and
tossed it past the dog. Old Cookie seemed to find new life as she
sprinted after it.

Millie straddled the banana seat and took off down the lane.
The machine shed was on the opposite side of the street; she slowed to
look for traffic before continuing across. Her bike was too big for her
to reach the ground while she was in the seat so she lunged forward
when she stopped to catch the ground with her free foot to keep the
bike upright. As she looked back over her shoulder, Cookie, with the
yellow tennis ball, trotted out into the street and collided with a faded
green pickup truck.

Amelia's eyes blinked open. The bright fluorescent light stung her eyes. It was as if someone had just awoken her from a long sleep by flipping on the lights. She tried to squint to keep out the light but she couldn't. She tried to raise her hand to shield the light but she couldn't. "Where am I and why am I restrained?" she thought. She heard a beeping noise in the distance. She heard an intercom paging "Doctor Whitehall to E.R." "Ok. I'm in a hospital... but why?" She heard a noise like a chair sliding on a hard surface. She heard a heavy sigh and then she heard...

"Esther – you still awake?" It was her father's voice. Amelia wanted to speak but she couldn't make a sound.

"I don't think I've slept since Friday." she heard her mother say in a voice that sounded weakened and tired. "Every time I close my eyes, I see Millie being wheeled in on that gurney. Harlen, I didn't even recognize her. They had to tell me it was her." Her mother began to cry.

"Honey I am so sorry I wasn't with you when you got the call about the accident."

"Accident" Amelia thought. "Ok, I was in an accident. When? Friday? What day is it now?"

"I'm sorry you had to go through any part of this ordeal alone. Euless wouldn't let me drive myself to the hospital... he's a good friend ya know. Said he talked to the farmer that was driving the harvester. He's pretty shook up. His neighbors are finishing his field for him. Euless said all the neighbors are pitching in to take care of us. They should have the corn out of the fields by the end of the week. Carl and Ed are putting some of it up; the rest is going to the co-op." Esther's weeping didn't change. Harlen went on talking about the farm and the neighbors because it was the only subject he could let himself think about.

"We should be able to get another cutting on the hay this year. That'll help with…"

Esther broke into his private conversation. "You realize we are going to have to sell the farm Harlen. She's going to require some specialized care and our insurance isn't going to pick up but 70%." Harlen stared down at his hands, picking nervously at the dry thickened skin around his weathered finger nails. In a stronger voice Esther asserted to her husband, "Dear, if she makes it out of this coma she'll be a quadriplegic, she won't be able to dress herself, bathe herself or feed herself. We *are* going to need some help."

"Quadriplegic!" Amelia screamed in her mind. She panicked and began to cry. Tears filled her eyes and her throat. In an attempt to swallow them she began to choke. The gurgling sound in her airway brought both parents to their feet.

Chapter 4

The trauma team snapped on latex gloves; it was late and the night had been unusually busy. "I guess they'll keep him on life support until they can find someone to claim him, but that guy's brains are hamburger. I'd like to see how his opponent looks. Street fighters – man talk about a bunch of brain fried individuals. They got no brains to start with and even less when they're done." The attending physician was referring to the John Doe that had been brought into the emergency room an hour earlier.

"What's the story here?" asked the beleaguered young doctor as he looked down at the next possible cadaver of the night.

"Bike accident," answered the EMT, "hit a deer."

Dirk's consciousness was intermittent and dream like. He heard the officer tell the doctor that they needed a blood sample before they administered treatment so they could run a drug/alcohol screen.

"You bastard," Dirk wanted to say, had he been capable, "if you want my fucking blood you can go scrape it off the fucking street." The needle was in his arm. His head swooned, "If I die of blood loss I swear I will come back and haunt you."

The surgeon looked down at Dirk then nodded to the anesthesiologist. His eyes smiled sarcastically. He waved and said "nighty-night" as Dirk's muddled world faded to black.

In the blackness Dirk moved at first in solitude toward a commanding beacon. Where the light created shadow he was met by another figure. Fully illuminated, Evron and Dirk exchanged a bewildered look and continued moving instinctively toward their destination. They stood, each in their own parallel line behind others who preceded them. The subtle lighting iridescently diffused the whiteness of the room giving the floors, walls and ceilings, if there were walls and ceilings, an intangible quality. The smell was of fresh baked bread. The silence was not reverent or fearful, but introspective. The line inched slowly forward and those at the front of the line faded then disappeared into a gauzy cloud.

Dirk and Evron stood in their own parallel lines flanked by others in their lines; all appeared healthy and normal, bewildered and obedient. Dirk stood on two legs, his wounds completely gone. Evron appeared clean and unscathed by the previous events of the night. His name was softly announced: Evron James Brown, age forty-two, cause of death head trauma. He advanced and was consumed by the fog.

As if a rope had been fastened to his posterior belt loop, Dirk was violently tugged. He stumbled and regained his balance. Others behind him in line stepped aside. Repeatedly, he was jerked and wrenched backward. The light faded away as he fell back and down into the black tunnel.

There was a bright light at the end of the tunnel; a harsh, blinding, antiseptic white light and the smell of disinfectant.

Chapter 5

The acrid odor of disinfectant coated her nostrils so that all she could smell, all she would be able to smell for hours was the stench of sanitizing, anti-viral, hospital grade disinfectant. "Wump, wump, wump, wump," her hospital bed made the noise as she was transported through halls. "Wump… one, two… wump… one, two," she paced off the rhythm in her head. Amelia kept her eyes closed. The conveyor belt of fluorescent bulbs made her nauseous. When the wump slowed "one, two, three," she began to hear other sounds; typical hospital static she'd become used to over the past weeks. "Wump… one, two, three, four." She heard something quite different.

"Oh Billy, Oh Millie, criminally insane………… All chopped up and sealed tight in baggies, I guess love makes you do funny things…Oh, Billy, Oh Millie, criminally insane. Oh Billie – Oh Millie. Bom… Bom… Bom."

At the far end of a hospital room a girl dressed in black pounded an air guitar and rocked her head to the music of Alice Cooper. Pages of a sketch pad papered the wall surrounding her with pencil drawings of expressive faces and candid moments. Her back was to Amelia and her entourage as they entered the room. Esther and Harlen watched as the orderly put their daughter's bed in place and attached the bells and whistles to the accompanying machines. A nurse approached the young rocker and lifted her head phones. "Kimberly, turn it down or I will take it away… again. This is your new roommate – Amelia."

The girl turned and swung her legs easily over the side of the bed. She leaned to get a look at Amelia. Kimberly Shobek wore pale ivory foundation, black lipstick and heavy black eye liner. "Kimmy," she said to the new girl.

Amelia's head was lolled to one side, by no force of her own, and she looked into Kimmy's eyes. "Dear God … my roommate… is Satan," she thought sardonically.

"She don't say much does she?" Kimmy said. Then she slid back on her pillow, replaced her headphones and closed her eyes.

Esther and Harlen exchanged a look. They wished they could have afforded a private room. Neither had missed a day in the four weeks that Amelia had been in the hospital. Harlen leaned against the wall, his arms folded resolutely and unsociably across his chest. Hospitals made him uncomfortable. It was too clean, too cramped, too structured and filled with sickness and death. Harlen was a farmer. He appreciated the simple cycle of life; cultivate, sew, nurture and harvest. If one of his cattle became sick it was culled from the herd and destroyed. It was simply the cycle of life.

Unsure that his daughter could actually understand him, he said very little to her. His physical presence was all he could offer and he quietly prayed, from behind the sports section, that Amelia could somehow grab onto his strength. At the opposite end of the spectrum was Esther, a supportive, intelligent, loving and social wife and mother who now babbled incessantly with inane, infantile chatter.

"Alright dear, your dad and I need to be going home now, but you'll be ok here. The nurses will be in to check on you soon. You be good sweetie." She leaned over and kissed Amelia's cheek. Amelia thought to herself, "Just shoot me... would someone please just shoot me now." "She is going to drive me insane!" she screamed in her head.

Amelia could see Kimmy's black stocking feet bouncing to the beat of music. She heard a faint tinny sounding rhythm and assumed correctly that Kimmy was jamming again to her headphones. Kimmy belted out more lyrics, "We're all crazy, we're all crazy."

"Yup... I'd agree with that. What are you like a Ozzy Osbourne groupie?" Amelia thought. Just then Kimmy flipped off her headphones and leaned into Amelia's view.

"It's Alice Cooper," she said. "You know most people think he's just some whacked dude on drugs. They're wrong. The Hey Stoopid lyrics are so damn good! That song is all about how *asinine* it is to use drugs. And the album," she went on excitedly, "wow, I think it opens the eyes of people who feel sorry for themselves. It should be played every day on every radio station, maybe then people wouldn't wallow in their own self-pity." She composed herself with an exaggerated deep breath. "Ok so what's your deal? Are you stupid or brain damaged or can you actually understand me?"

"Man, I'd like to damage you. Would you shut up and leave me alone," Amelia thought.

"Alright – Can you blink your eyes?" She said.

Amelia was shocked. "Yeah... I can blink." She blinked.

"Ok – once for yes, twice for no. Do you understand me?"

Amelia blinked once. She didn't have a thought in her head at this point only elation at being able to communicate.

"Was that just a fluke?"

Two blinks. Amelia was so happy she wondered if tears were spilling down her face.

"Ok, great! I think we can get along. So what do you think of my music. Do you like it?" Amelia didn't blink. "I'll take that as a polite no. Look, I'm really not this weird, I mean I do like Alice Cooper but I don't always dress like this. It's Halloween and my friends and I have always had a tradition of dressing up and hitting the garage bands. I won't be going of course but they'll be by before they head out."

"Thank you," Amelia thought, "You're weird, but thanks for talking to me, for treating me like a person."

The knock at the door came from a young woman with very red hair – not like a Clairol natural auburn, but a red so glaring that it distracted your attention from any of her other features. She wore an extremely short black leather miniskirt over torn fishnet stockings and a mint green rubber or plastic vest that squeezed her young breasts into an unnatural and ill proportioned shape. Her nose and her eyebrow jewelry were gold studs. Façade aside, she was a strikingly beautiful young woman.

"Hey Margie. How ya doing?" Kimmy asked excitedly.

"Hey Kimmy K. How's it hanging?" Margie's heavy pallid makeup and excessive dark eyeliner and shadow matched Kimmy's. "You feeling ok?"

"I'd feel a lot better if you could sneak me out of here... where is every one?" Kimmy looked around Margie to the door.

Margie looked at the floor. Then she looked up and said in a fake cheery voice. "Trash and Jo Jo are in the car. Trash hates hospitals Jo stayed to keep him company. Mickey and Spoof are gonna meet us at Hell's Kitchen pretty soon. I can't stay, everyone's waiting on me. I brought you a new demo from the Booger's." She handed the tape to Kimmy. "They're starting to sound pretty good.

They all say to say hey…." She hesitated and looked around the room nervously. Her uneasy gaze was snared momentarily by the unexpected site of the inert and disfigured roommate.

"Look, I really gotta get," she said with a genuine apologetic tone.

"No, hey don't sweat it... I hate hospitals too. Don't worry about it. Hey, rock hard tonight," Kimmy said, still sounding up beat.

"I'll call ya soon," Margie said as she sheepishly left the room.

There was a moment of silence before Amelia heard the sound of the cassette case hitting the wall. A short time later she heard the muffled sound of pillow sobs.

* * *

Esther, with her hand over her mouth tried to stifle her sobs. She sat cross legged on Amelia's bed at home. They had kept her room just as she left it when she went to school. It didn't make sense to change anything. Iowa State was only two hours from home and Amelia was back nearly every weekend.

In her free hand she held some photographs. When she was able to contain her sobs she flipped through them one by one. They were taken at a swim meet last fall, Millie's freshman year. It was one

27

of the few meets that Esther and Harlen had been able to attend. Most of the photos were of arms and splashes and colorful swim caps. She won the 400 meter free style that day. There were a few photographs of Amelia, thin, beautiful and muscular hugging her coach, her teammates, her father. She was beaming and beautiful.

Harlen had finished off the roll at home. There were two pictures of the dog sitting in the cab of the harvester and one candid photo of Esther pushing Amelia on the wooden swing behind the house. Amelia's bright and cheery eyes smiled back at Esther.

Her hands flew to her mouth to stifle a sob; the photos fell onto the bed.

***

The deck of cards landed squarely on Amelia's chest and Kimmy flopped casually onto Amelia's bed. "Ok, the game is five card draw are you familiar with it?" Kimmy wore comfy grey sweat pants and a wrinkled button down oxford. Her long chestnut hair was straight and clean. Her face had a fresh washed rosy glow and she smiled. She was twenty; she was thin and appeared to be in great shape. She was simply pretty.

Amelia wondered why Kimmy was there.

She blinked once. She wondered; had she been capable of speech, if she would have told Kimmy that she had been playing poker since she was seven.

Kimmy turned Amelia's face so that she looked straight at her. Then she scrunched the pillow on either side of her head to anchor her there. She dealt two piles of five cards then held Amelia's cards so that only Amelia could see them. She waited a minute and then pointed to the top of the first card in her hand.

"Let me know which cards you want to hold. This one?"

Amelia blinked twice and Kimmy discarded the indicated playing card. She moved through the hand one by one.

"Ok you threw out three cards – doesn't sound like a great hand."

She dealt three replacement cards and added them to Amelia's hand. She held them up for Amelia to view for a few seconds. "Ok, remember them while I go through mine." After looking at her own card she said, "I'm taking two."

"Now we each have twenty of these little goldfish crackers." She held up the Pepperidge Farm crackers for Amelia to see.

"Oh My God I'd love to eat one of those, I can't remember when I last tasted food," Amelia thought.

"You got first bid."

She blinked five times.

"Five; wow gutsy move. I'll see your five and raise you five. Now if you want to call, just close your eyes for like three seconds."

Amelia did.

Kimmy added Amelia's five additional goldfish to the pile on the sheets and flipped over both sets of cards.

Amelia could tell she had won by Kimmy's expression. Kimmy showed Amelia her own cards. "A pair of jacks." Amelia had held a suited Jack/Queen and caught the straight.

She was so thrilled to have someone interact with her; someone who treated her like a whole person and not an invalid. Tears puddled at the edge of the tape that held an abundance of gauze to her cheek. Kimmy snatched a Kleenex from the side table to dab at the tears. Next to the box of Kleenex was a picture of Amelia, her mother, father and bi-colored border collie. She guessed that it must have been Amelia. It did not at all resemble the disfigured woman before her. She realized that her eyes lingered there too long and she quickly recovered. "That must be your dog," she said reaching for the picture. "Wow, he's adorable." She replaced the picture and wiped Amelia's tears.

"So you're pretty lucky at this game huh?" She dealt out two more hands and repeated the process. She held up the cards in front of Amelia and discarded as indicated.

There were three cards discarded and Kimmy tried to count them. She said "two, seven," she started again "two, toes," Sternly she corrected herself, clenched shut her eyes, shook her head and concentrated on the cards. "Three cards," she said finally." After dealing out three new cards, she tried to place them in her hand but the cards fell onto the sheet.

Kimmy's eyes locked on Amelia's with a silent, painful pleading request that she knew Amelia could not fulfill. She grabbed hold of the side rail of the bed and curled into a trembling ball. By the erratic movement of the bed, Amelia could tell that Kimmy shuddered fiercely. She heard her low and painful cries, "Owee, owee, owee, oh my God, owee, please help. Please stop. Oh shit, oh shit," Kimmy whimpered weakly.

Amelia was helpless and terrified. She screamed for help in her head then she began to cry. The tears streamed down her face and onto her pillow. The moisture pooled in her throat; she could not clear it. Her monitor sounded as her heart rate soared. A nurse entered then retreated quickly to the hall to call for assistance. The orderly, a clean shaven bear of a young man with strong hairy arms, ran into the room behind her and both tried to lift Kimmy from Amelia's bed. It eventually took three people to tear Kimmy's hand from the bed rail. Amelia could see Kimmy's tightly clenched fist where it was cemented to the bed. In the curve between her thumb and index finger of her right hand Amelia saw a trembling butterfly, not a tattoo, but a latte colored quivering birthmark. Like the gong of an old farm dinner bell, the sound reverberated through the room as Kimmy's hand was ripped free of the bedrail. They placed her back in her bed, strapped her torso down with leather straps and put several injections in her IV port. Kimmy's knees were still tight against her chest while she was flat on her back. The whimpering subsided. After a few minutes her legs began to slowly uncurl. Heavy sand bags were brought in and laid across her ankles and thighs. When the nurse left, the orderly stayed in a chair beside Kimmy's bed for what seemed like an hour.

When Esther and Harlen entered the room Amelia heard them before she saw them. Esther gasped… "Whoa!" her father said. The orderly explained, "She has advanced progressive MS. This is one of her bad days. The sand bags help to stretch out her muscles. The tie down is there in case the sandbags don't work and she spasms again."

Esther addressed Harlen with a hushed but audible voice. "Katherine Sparks has MS." Either the name didn't register with him or the shock of the current scene rendered the comment insignificant. "From Church," Esther continued, "but she sure doesn't look like that." They remained firmly entrenched in their position, fixated on the discomforting site but unable to look away.

He attempted to help them better understand. "MS symptoms vary from person to person based on the diseases category and the location of the central nervous system damage. They can be as mild as occasional muscle cramps and dizziness or, like Kimmy here, as severe as spasticity, seizures and tremors. In most cases the disease doesn't hit until after the age of twenty, but sometime we see kids."

Nodding toward Kimmy he continued, "She's been coming in here since I started – that was eight years ago so she's had it at least since the age of twelve. The disease goes through periods of remissions and relapses but her attacks are becoming more frequent and violent. The nerves in her brain and spinal cord are progressively deteriorating." He paused to let them absorb the barrage of information.

"Is there anything they can do?" Esther sympathetically inquired.

"There's no treatment for it yet but medication can, in most cases, slow the disease. Kimmy's here as part of a study for a new procedure. Several weeks ago a portion of her bone marrow was extracted and treated; then she received low doses of chemo and radiation to kill off her immune system. That's the important part. An MS body's white blood cells attack the myelin covering the Central Nervous System, that's how the damage occurs. The extracted marrow was replaced with the hopes that the newly produced white cells won't be destructive. It's produced some pretty good results in some cases, usually for younger, less disabled people. For some, their MS returns, sometimes more progressively. It's a risky procedure; the verdict is still out on how it's affecting Kimmy."

"Is she in pain?" asked Esther.

"Not anymore, not with the amount of painkillers they just pumped in her. I doubt she'd feel it if we cut her legs clean off." He wrote more notes in Kimmy's chart then excused himself.

"MS?" thought Amelia, "Muscular sc… no Multiple Sclerosis. That's it. Damn, this is what it does to you? Poor girl."

Esther stepped into Amelia's view. She bent down close to her face and said in her slow and child taming voice "Let's just turn you away from that sight sweetie. I know you don't want to look at that do ya now. Are you having a good day?"

She winced inside at the way her mother spoke to her. She thought to herself, "I actually was having one of the best days I've had since the accident up until about a half hour ago. Even though I can't move or talk or run away from your annoyingly patronizing voice, I am still having a better day than Kimmy."

Harlen sat in his usual chair and flapped open the newspaper. He was settling in for another few hours at the hospital. This had been his routine every day. Esther sat beside Amelia's bed and talked for two hours about trivia. Today's trivia included what she cooked for supper, the proper way to track the number of stitches while crocheting an afghan and how many and what types of birds visited her feeder that morning.

Amelia closed her eyes as her mom continued to rattle on. She thought of a morning last spring when she sat with her mother at the kitchen table drinking coffee. The sparrows flitted in and out of the bird feeder while they talked at length about the similarities and differences in strong female role models like Aung San Suu Kyi, Madeline Albright and Margaret Thatcher. Of the three very different women, Amelia recalls her mother saying, "Albright and Thatcher struggled to become a political figure while Suu Kyi was destined through a family dynasty. Thatcher was a terrific leader and given the opportunity so too would be Suu Kyi and Albright. But Suu Kyi sits under house arrest in Burma for violating her exile status and Albright is shackled by the US constitution which prohibits foreign born citizens from becoming President."

When Amelia opened her eyes the memory was gone but her mother's trivial babbling continued. She was staring straight ahead at an oversized calendar on the wall. Courtesy of Lucas Co-op, November was a picture of a hay field in harvests. The date was Tuesday, November first. She began singing to herself to drown her mother's voice from her head. "Ninety-nine bottles of beer on the wall, Ninety-nine bottles of beer…."

She opened her eyes again and the scene was the same; her father in the same chair, her mother sitting beside her, but her father was wearing a different ball cap and her mother a different sweater. The date on the calendar in front of her bed was Thursday, November third. A large handmade greeting card was taped to the wall beside the calendar. "Get Well Soon" from the Trinity Lutheran Sunday school class. It was signed in crayon by every child.

"Two bottles of beer on the wall, … One bottle of beer on the wall, one bottle of beer, take one down and pass it around no more bottles of beer on the wall….." There was silence. "Oh thank God she has finally stopped talking… she must be asleep," Amelia thought. Then she heard the toilet flush.

"Now then sweetie pie would you like me to turn your head this way so you can see out the window for a while? I sure bet you would. Now isn't that better?" Her mother dripped the words sweetly from her tongue.

From the next bed she heard Kimmy say in a soft but exasperated tone, "Oh for God sakes… she's crippled, she's not retarded."

"I beg your pardon?" Esther shot back indignantly. Although he cracked a wry smile from behind the headlines, Harlen's paper didn't flinch.

"You're treating her like a child and you are driving her nuts. Ask her. One blink is yes, two is no. Ask her!" She barked in exasperation. "Because I know you're driving me nuts."

The Des Moines Register abruptly dropped to the floor as Harlen nearly leapt to Amelia's bedside next to Esther. Both stared with anxious anticipation. Her father said "Amelia, hon, do you think you mother is treating you like a child?

One Blink.

Esther's hand flew to her mouth. Harlen's relief softened the lines in his face which had aged him so quickly in recent weeks, "Do you want to hear more trivia about those damned birds?"

Two Blinks.

36

Esther's free hand flew to her mouth where it covered the first as if she needed both to contain the sound of her excitement and relief. Harlen laughed, "That's my girl!" He hugged his wife and held her tightly while her joyful tears dampened even his cotton undershirt. "Ohhhh, *Thank you Kimmy!*" Amelia sighed in her mind. A tear ran down her cheek.

Chapter 6

He removed a single tear from his cheek with his free hand, in the other he held a small piece of paper. The YMCA logo was faded, handwritten in pink ink was Millie 555-7117. Alex sat on the edge of his bed and remembered the coach's words. "Amelia Specter won't be joining us for practice today. In all likelihood she won't be joining us again ever." He hesitated and swallowed hard. "I got a call from her father over the weekend; she was in a very bad car accident Friday night. She's in critical condition at Mercy Hospital in Des Moines. Visitors are currently restricted to her immediate family but if she," he corrected himself, "when she regains consciousness visitors will be welcome."

Alex refolded the slip of paper and placed it back in the old cigar box with other mementos he valued. He sat cross legged on his bed staring into the box at the folded paper. He closed his eyes and remembered....

Amelia was younger, sixteen then, already beautiful. Her blond hair, still damp from the swim, hung as a ponytail stuck out of the back of an ISU ball cap. She searched her gym bag for change as she stood in front of the vending machine, nothing. Her head slumped and she sighed heavily. From over her shoulder a dollar bill appeared.

"My treat," said the young handsome figure behind her. His black hair was slick with water and he smelled of chlorine.

"Thanks." She inserted the bill and removed a bag of pretzels. Returning the change, she said "Millie" as she stuck out her hand. He took it and held it.

Amelia was used to the formalities of greeting adults rather than peers. She had spent most of her life around people who were older and had few, maybe no real friends her own age.

Alex stared at her hand and turned it over caressing the top then looked into her eyes and smiled. Amelia was inwardly surprised at her own reaction. She felt her cheeks grow hot and her stomach tighten. Alex released her hand. "Billy, my name, it's Billy." So, looks like we're stuck here until this storm lets up. I've never seen you here before."

Amelia explained that her parents were vacationing in Mexico and she was here for the weekend with her .... They sat at the break room table detailing the insignificant trivia of their lives, each giving only small details to be reciprocated by the other. The rhetoric didn't matter. It was the chemistry that made the evening interesting.

Hours had elapsed; the snow had turned to freezing rain which formed an icy curtain against the window. They passed the time with table top football as they took turns making brief contact with their hands, legs, arms and generally any body part that would allow seemingly incidental contact.

Amelia stood at the windows of the YMCA cafeteria, through cupped hands she peered out through the prism of ice into the dark and shimmering night. Alex stood close behind her, his thighs touching the back of hers. His cheek lightly brushed hers as he too tried to look through the veiled widow. Her silky hair, now dry, nuzzled her shoulders like an affectionate feline begging to be stroked.

Amelia held her breath; her heart raced in her chest. His body touching hers so boldly gripped her with an emotion she could neither define nor react to. Alex wanted to linger but he was surprised by his forward behavior and uncomfortably stepped back. "I'm gonna check with the desk to see if they have any idea when this thing will let up."

When Alex had gone, Amelia turned her back to the window, she released a long held breath and with her bottom lip blew a cooling gulp of air onto her face while she fanned herself. She raised her long hair and pressed the back of her neck to the cool glass.

He returned carrying pillows and blankets. "Ron, at the desk gave me these. He said this isn't gonna let up for a while. He also said the ….." the room went dark... "power might go out." They stumbled forward in the dark looking for each other then bumped hard. They both laughed.

"Let's sit over against the wall," Amelia said.

"Which wall?"

She took his hand and he followed her in the dark. Unable to see his face, Amelia felt more relaxed. The darkness provided a false anonymity which allowed her inhibitions to drop away. She brought the hand she was holding to her lips and kissed it. His free hand felt the warmth of her flushed cheek as he gently stroked it. He leaned into her and kissed her lips as the pillows and blankets fell to the floor.

The dim flashing yellow light of a snow plow beaconed through dwindling flurries as Alex and Amelia stood under the awning of the YMCA entrance. Her Chevette idled a few feet away, barely discernible in make, model or color through eight inches of snow and ice that covered all but the windows. Amelia pressed a folded piece of paper into his hands, kissed his cheek and headed for the car. He unfolded the paper as she pulled away; Millie 555-7117, was scrawled in pink ink.

He folded the paper placed it in the breast pocket of his down filled coat. The lining was torn away from the pocket and the note slipped past the pocket, lost in the fine feathers.

Two years later Alex stood in the hallway of his grandmother's rent controlled building holding a cardboard box full of clothes, two additional boxes with books and other items that had filled his room sat next to him on the floor as he waited for the elevator.

"Billy that coat's just too small for you," His grandma said, lifting the heavy winter coat from a box on the floor. "You can't be going off to college with something that fits you that way. Throw that there thing on the goodwill pile down near the door on your way out. Someone here in this building can get some use out of it."

His Grandma had raised him since he was eight years old and she was the only person who called him by his middle name, his grandfather's name. Alex had respected and admired his Grandfather. He crushed the coat in his hands to see if he had left anything in the pockets and felt the tenuous give of a folded piece of paper. He fished deep into the lining of the coat and pulled out the note written in pink ink on a YMCA scratch pad. The elevator opened but Alex didn't move. He stared at the paper. It closed again.

Chapter 7

The elevator doors opened and Jimmy Shobek slowly shuffled out and down the long corridor toward his sister's room. He was hung over from the night before. Although he had showered, the smell of Admiral Nelson's spiced rum emanated from his pores. He turned into Kimmy's room and stared in disbelief at what he saw. A small child, a girl seven or eight years old with shiny black hair, lay motionless; a maze of tubes and hoses in her arms, nose and throat. His head throbbed and the room seemed to move under his feet. He reached for the wall to steady himself then eased into a chair and sat with his head in his hands rubbing hard at his brow to push back the percussion of the monitors.

Beep. Beep. Beep. Beep. An alarm on one of the girl's monitors sounded. It screeched relentlessly and painfully loud in his ears; amplifying his already pounding headache. No one came to check on the alert so Jimmy went into the hall. He looked at the number on the room…3573. Kimmy's room was 5573, two floors up.

At the nurse's station, a young woman was having a semiprofessional phone conversation with a colleague. Her smock was speckled with miniature Garfields. A small fuzzy Garfield the cat figure was clipped to her stethoscope which was looped in typical medical fashion around her neck.

"Hey, there is an alarm going off in 3573."

"Oh, thanks." She flipped a button and the alarm went silent.

He expected she would get up and go check on the girl, or call another nurse to go but she went back to her phone call. He sighed heavily in response to the nurse's apparent apathy and continued past the station to the elevators. While he waited, he heard the alarm sound again. The interminable beeping tugged at his conscience and as the doors parted, Jimmy returned to 3573. There appeared to have been no response to the alarm. He walked over to the small girl and studied her cherubic face. She seemed lifeless except that her chest rose and fell. Her hair was shorter on the left side of her head in a pattern which extended from above the ear and continued to a place hidden by the pillow; obviously shaved, not recently, but not long ago. The hair was less than a half inch long there. Aside from that she appeared normal.

The alarm continued. He reached down to the bedside and pressed the CALL FOR HELP button on the controls. After a minute or two the Garfield adorned nurse arrived.

With the press of a button, the alarm stopped. She adjusted the nasal cannula in the girl's nose and spoke while she worked. "The pulse-ox alarm sounds when levels drop below ninety. The nasal cannula slipped out of her nose so she wasn't getting the air flow she needed."

"Will that hurt her?" asked Jimmy.

The nurse looked at him with a puzzled expression. "You know she has no higher brain function, right?"

"No, I'm sorry I didn't know that."

"Are you a relative?"

"No, I just walked into the wrong room. My sister is in 5573, a couple floors up. Guess I wasn't paying attention when I got off the elevator."

"I thought that it was odd. She hasn't had a single visitor since she's been here."

"What happened to her?"

"She was in a car accident about 6 weeks ago. Her grandparents, who were her legal guardians, were both killed. Poor kid's parents were killed in a car accident a year ago. She suffered severe head trauma and hasn't shown any signs of higher brain activity. The neurologist said she'll never recover. This is as good as she'll get. They've recommended she be taken off life supports. She has an uncle in Georgia, her only living relative, but he can't bear to pull the plug. Poor girl." The nurse reached out a hand and touched the soft little cheek in sympathy.

Her pager hummed on her waistband. She checked it and headed for the door. Jimmy asked just before the nurse reached the door, "What's her name?"

"Hope." she answered with an apologetic look at the child.

***

The elevator door opened again and Jimmy stepped onto the fifth floor. He heard the low, polite conversation with a reference to "the good Lord" and stepped back to look again at the room number. Tentatively he entered the room which was filled with conservatively dressed women in comfortable shoes. Even more to his surprise was the disfigured and partially bandaged Amelia.

"Can I help you?" Harlen enquired.

"I'm looking for Kimmy Shobek."

Harlen pointed to the far side of the room where Jimmy's sister reclined in her bed, head phones blaring and eyes closed. He lifted the head set from her ears and her eyes shot open with a reproachful glare.

In recognition she smiled brightly. "Hey! Where you been? It's so good to see you!" He hugged her with some reserved distance. Conversation was difficult with all the other talk in the room.

Kimmy snapped, "Hey! My turn for a guest! I'm entitled to one too ya know. *And*, I'm sure Amelia has heard enough about Aunt Faye's *bunion* and Bridgette's seven puppies."

The guests, members of Esther's prayer group who had come with prayers and local gossip, looked embarrassed. Each felt compelled to touch Amelia in parting as if by some miracle Amelia would be healed. Esther went into the hall with the women. Harlen stayed and continued reading the paper.

Jimmy and Kimmy witnessed the ritual and exchanged laughing glances at the spectacle. He reached for a recently vacated chair and pulled it to Kimmy's bedside then eased his unstable frame into the still warm vinyl padding. Kimmy notice the effort in his motion and the familiar smell of the morning after.

"Dad says hi," he said when the room was finally silent. "He'll be up to visit soon."

"Soon as pigs fly," she quipped. Then she wished she hadn't. "I'm sorry Jimmy. I know hospitals are a tough place for you and Dad. Thank you for coming." Kimmy had made note of a few details upon his arrival. First, it was mid-morning on a Monday; also, he was unshaven and smelled of cheap whiskey and cheaper cigarettes. "Tough night?" she asked.

"Yeah, I lost my job." He didn't tell her it was because he was caught drinking at work.

"You could get one here at the hospital. They could use your breath to sterilize surgical instruments." She smiled to lighten the mood.

He hung his head and laughed insincerely. The laugh turned to cough, the cough of a persistent smoker. Reflexively, he reached for the pack of Dorals in his shirt pocket; then shook his head as if to clear the thought and pushed the pack back into his pocket.

"I'm gonna quit these things sis. When this new treatment works and you walk out of here for good, these damned things," he patted his shirt pocket, "are going in the trash."

"I wish you'd do it for yourself and not for me Jimmy. This drinkin and smokin is gonna put you in an early grave bro." Again she tried to sound upbeat, even when issuing the worn out reprimand.

He stared at his dirty tennis shoes for a long time before Kimmy put a hand on his knee and changed the subject. "So, how's Dad?"

"Good, he left Thursday to haul a load to Philadelphia then he's heading to Dallas. He'll probably try to get something back here by midweek so he should be able to make it up here in a week or so."

They both sat quietly for a moment then Kimmy gave him the excuse to leave that he wouldn't make himself. "You better go get the Sunday paper while there's still some on the stands. I'm sure you'll have a job by the end of the week." He stood to leave.

"Maybe a smoke shop or a liquor store is hiring," he said with a grin. She was glad to see him smile. He kissed the top of her head and ruffled her hair. "Be good kiddo." He winked at her as he left the room.

When he was a few steps beyond the door he stopped and leaned against a wall. With his eyes shut he took a long deep breath and exhaled the weight of the visit. Alex Garreth stood before him when Jimmy opened his eyes. Alex was looking at the hand written name plates on the door just past Jimmy's left shoulder.

"You lost?" Jimmy asked.

"No," said Alex.

"You going in?"

"No," Alex said with some hesitation. They both walked to the elevator. On the way, Alex left a vase of pink carnations at the nurse's station. "Can you give these to Amelia Specter?" The card read: I'm so sorry, Alex William Garreth, "Billy".

Chapter 8

The low voltage hum of the florescent light above Amelia's
bed was made loud by the silence of the room. No visitors, no music.
A long time seemed to pass undisturbed until Kimmy appeared next to
Amelia's bedside, her IV poll in tow. "Hey girl, you awake?" she
whispered. Amelia's eyes snapped open and her left arm nearly
jumped off the bed.

"Holy shit!" said Kimmy. "Did you do that on purpose?"

Two blinks, No.

"Try!" Kimmy was excited for her friend's possible progress.
"Nothing, huh?"

Two blinks.

"We'll maybe it's something. I'll tell your nurse. Did I wake
you?"

Two blinks.

"Hey I have some grape jelly from lunch. You want me to put some on your tongue, see if you can taste it? You gotta be starving."

One blink. "Oh God I'd love some real food. I'd love to taste anything. You could put dirt on my tongue and I'd be happy to taste it." Amelia thought.

One blink. One blink.

"Ok.. I get it," she laughed a small laugh. "You're funny." She opened the small jelly jar and scooped a very small amount on her finger. Then she opened Amelia's mouth and placed a spot on her tongue. Kimmy wiped her hand on Amelia's bed sheet.

"Can you taste it?"

Two blinks.

"Bummer."

Amelia made a new eye gesture – quick, long, quick.

"That's new. Is that thanks?"

One blink.

"Got it." Kimmy leaned across Amelia's face and gave the opposite eye gesture. Long, quick, long. "You're welcome," she said.

She gently turned Amelia's head to face her own bed then backed away to her bed dragging her pole. "Sorry I got to sit down, my legs are cramping. Did you see my brother?"

One blink.

"Cute isn't he?" She paused. "I mean, well he looks a lot better when he's not hung over. You're wondering why I don't have many visitors. My dad and my brother are all I got for family. Mom died when I was pretty little. She did a lot of drugs and it damaged her kidneys. She was in and out of the hospital a lot, so they tell me. I was like three when she died. I don't remember her. I guess that when she was home she was so whacked out on pain killers that she couldn't form rational sentences. So this disease I have reminds Jimmy and Dad of Mom. It's hard for them ya know, it's just gonna get harder too. They don't want…" She reconsidered her words. "They can't take care of me when I get cramped up. I overheard the nurses say that if this treatment doesn't work, they'll have to move me to a *"facility"*. Over my dead body!"

"I guess it's no coincidence that we're roommates. If you didn't have such doting parents you'd end up in a facility too. I'd prefer that option to listening endlessly to your mother carry on both sides of a conversation for the rest of my life. Dear God, does that woman ever take a breath?" Kimmy flinched inwardly and again she wanted to take back what she said. "Sorry, sometimes I let my elephant mouth overload my parakeet ass."

Amelia closed her eyes. She allowed herself to imagine what it would be like at home; her mother and her father lowering her naked body into a bath tub, her father looking away uncomfortably, her mother struggling alone to dress Amelia's limp body. She pictured herself sitting motionless in a wheel chair, her disfigured head strapped firmly to a support, parked alone beneath the big maple tree in the back yard, the old wooden swing swaying in the breeze, her fat fawn and white boxer sitting at her feet with a tennis ball in his mouth pleading with her to play fetch.

A glass fell from Kimmy's side table and broke on the floor. Amelia opened her eyes as Kimmy reached for the call button; the muscles on her arm spasmed rapidly. Her face grimaced with pain.

"Sorry," said Kimmy "for what I said about your Mom. I didn't mean it. I'd give anything to have someone care that much about me."

Quick, long, quick – "thanks."

The nurse entered the room with a concoction of pain killers and muscle relaxers and pushed it into Kimmy's IV. "It'll kick in pretty quick," she said to Kimmy who was sweating and trembling severely.

Very shortly thereafter Kimmy and Amelia slept.

***

Kimmy drove a shiny red Mustang convertible; Amelia, healthy and vibrant, rode shot gun. The music blared Billie and Mille on the radio as the wind tossed their hair. The day was sunny, warm and beautiful. In the distance a man stood at the roadside. As they got closer it was Alex holding pillows and blankets folded in his arms. When they pulled aside him he was naked from the waist up, his hair wet, a towel was draped over his shoulder. "Come on in girls, the water is warm."

Amelia responded in a mechanical voice, "You were supposed to call me. That was the plan." The words came from an optically operated speech machine. Amelia stared at the reflection of her mangled face in the side view mirror.

She was startled awake both by the dream and by the conversation in the room. A vase of pink carnations blocked her view of Kimmy and her guests.

Chapter 9

"We'll send this sample over to the lab to see if the bone marrow transplant has had any effect on your neuro blockers," the doctor said as the technician labeled the blood sample and left the room. "In some cases the effects have been substantial and immediate, reversing the effect of the disease totally. In other cases results have been moderate and in some it has been totally unsuccessful. This procedure is still very new Kimberly, so I don't want you to get your hopes up, ok? When you are done with physical therapy, they'll bring you to my office to discuss the results. I'll see you in a few hours."

The doctor left the room as the orderly prepared her wheelchair. "Your chariot, Princess Kimberly," said the young orderly who had been her transport now for almost a month.

She smiled at him. "Once around the park Jeeves."

When she was settled into her chair she said to Amelia, "Wow, nice flowers. I guess you're someone special now huh?" She gave the two thumbs up signal to Amelia and gleamed with anticipation of her news. "My days here are numbered girl!"she said confidently. "I'll be walking out that door as soon as I get the good news. See ya in a few."

"Good luck Kimmy. Lord, give that girl a break. I hate to lose her company but she deserves a better fate," Amelia prayed.

Therapy was busy, most were regulars that Kimmy had seen before. Margaret, a single mother of two, was extremely obese and unemployed. She broke her back when she fell on the rain soaked steps of the unemployment office. The massive weight of her body compacted several of her vertebrae and damaged her spinal cord. Kimmy didn't know how long Margaret had been at Mercy but it was more than a month. Margaret nodded in Kimmy's direction while she shuffled down the red carpet with her new walker, an orderly on each side to catch her, just in case.

Kimmy slid up onto the leg extension bench and strapped her legs to the weighted bars. She looked across the room at a new patient; a man who she guessed to be in his mid-thirties. His arms and left leg bore angry pink skin, the sheath of a recent wound. The left leg was missing below the knee. He lifted a prosthetic leg from a box filled with packing peanuts and put the box on the floor. He turned the leg over in his hand to examine it. Then he set it on his lap and disapprovingly crossed his arms. His eyes met Kimmy's and she realized she had been staring. She did not look away.

"How do I know him?" she thought.

He turned his wheel chair abruptly and spilled the contents of the box next to him. Styrofoam packing peanuts scattered across the floor. Angrily, he lifted his prosthetic leg in his hand and smacked the box with it. The therapy room went silent at the noise and the mess. He put the leg back on his lap and wheeled heatedly out of the room.

Kimmy had worked up a sweat at her therapy session. She'd made an extra effort working more diligently than usual, as if a day's work could make a difference. The orderly parked her wheel chair in front of Dr. Kahn's desk. He wasn't in the room yet so the two waited silently for what were minutes but seemed hours. When the doctor entered the room he looked directly out the window. When he sat in his chair he looked at the pencil holder on his desk. When he cleared his throat and looked at Kimmy … she knew.

"Oh God… no," Amelia thought. "Poor kid." A tear ran down Amelia's cheek. There was not a sound from Kimmy as the once jovial orderly helped her quietly back into bed. Kimmy curled into a fetal ball and stared out the window in silence.

A hand reached across Amelia's face and wiped a tear from the angry wrinkled skin that used to be her cheek. "Hey hun, I see you got some more of your bandages off," her father said. He pulled a chair around and sat between the two beds blocking Amelia's view of Kimmy. "Are you having a sad day?"

"Every day," she wanted to reply. "One blink."

Harlen looked at the clock on the wall at the foot of Amelia's bed. "Millie, your Mom doesn't know I'm here. She thinks I'm running errands for the co-op so I can't stay long. I wanted to talk to you alone hon." He paused, took a breath to gather his courage and continued. "I want to do some straight shootin' with ya. I know we haven't told you much so, here's how it is, I know Mom keeps telling you you're gonna get better… and you will get better than you are right now, probably, but not much. When you're able to swallow solid food, they are going to let us take you home. That is as much as the doctors are expecting from you."

"Yeah, I figured as much, but it's still tough to hear you say it," she thought.

"There is this machine that can be fitted to a wheelchair that lets you use your eyes to type. I know you have all of your mental capacity so it's gotta be damn frustrating that you can't communicate. I got a job at the co-op and I'm gonna start saving every penny to get you that machine. Then I can save for plastic surgery. You would be amazed at what they can do."

"Don't worry Millie, we're gonna take care of you. I just don't want you to get any false hopes about making a full recovery," h emphasized. "Life is going to be different but it can still be good. I'll help you find a way to make it good."

Amelia shut her eyes and tried hard not to swallow the tears that had gathered at the back of her throat. Rather she would have them build and drool from her mouth than let on that she was regaining her ability to swallow.

Her father worked the land that his father and his grandfather had worked. Now he would give it all up to take care of her. She did not want to go home. She did not want to be "taken care of."

Kimmy didn't stir; not once, not for dinner, not for nurses, not for the rest of the day and into the night. They were like two rag dolls abandoned by children who no longer wanted to play. They lay motionless on damp, tear-filled pillows.

Chapter 10

"The plan that we talked about at Booger's party last fall… it's time. I know Margie, I've thought about it, *a lot*. Margie, you said you'd do this for me… you promised. We made a pact to take care of each other… please do this for me ok? …. No questions, no fuss. Ok?"

Amelia's heart raced in her chest. Tears streamed down her cheeks. Kimmy hung up the phone, lay back heavily on her bed and sighed. She stared with catatonic resolution, at the same sterile ceiling tiles that sealed both her fate and Amelia's.

With resolve and fortitude, Kimmy slowly slid her legs over the side of the bed. Her muscles were stiff and she was mentally and physically drained. She pushed the Demerol pump on her IV and looked over at Amelia who stared perpetually at the ceiling. Amelia's bandages were completely gone. The red and wrinkled skin formed angry scars across what once had been beautiful strong features. Kimmy shook her head in sympathy.

"How are you hanging in there girl? Looks like you'll be going home sometime soon." "Home, huh!" she grunted snidely. "I'm not going home. Dad said that he's lining up "care" for me. Well, I'm not going there either," she said firmly. "I just can't do it. I can't live if I can't live, ya know?" Her tone changed from snide to sincere, "If you wake up one morning soon and I'm not here... you've been a great listener, the best roommate I've ever had." She arched her back to stretch her tightening muscles and lifted her legs slowly back onto the bed then closed her eyes.

"Take me with you," Amelia pleaded. "Holy shit, *please* take me with you, take me with you! Take me with you!" she desperately repeated the mental phrase. "Is there any way I can tell you what I'm thinking? I know what you're planning. *You* don't want to go on because no one will take care of you. *I* don't want to because *everyone* will take care of me. Mom and Dad will bankrupt themselves trying to give me a life that is no life at all. I have no way to do it ... please help me!" she pleaded and sobbed in silence.

Amelia blinked twice.

"I'm so tired," said Kimmy.

Two blinks.

"Goodnight."

Two blinks.

***

The wheel chair crossed the threshold of the elevator and Amelia's head bobbled slightly. A cranial strap gave her support but was not snugly secured. Kimmy tipped the chair backward to help ease the jostling as she slid into position in the elevator. The elevator was empty.

Kimmy pushed the cold metal handicapped button and the hydraulic doors to the parking garage silently opened. They were unprepared for the cold winter air that stung their bodies through flimsy hospital gowns. "Holy sheep shit!" said Kimmy. "I've been in there so long I forgot it was winter." She leaned out of the doors looking for anyone who might see them leaving. No one was about so she pushed Amelia's chair down the long cold aisle of cars. The green aisle marker on the fourth floor said "D". The rusty, red, sun faded 1972 Super Beetle was easy to spot.

She opened the passenger door and parked Amelia next to it. Kimmy blew into her cold hands for warmth then fumbled with the buckles to free Amelia's stays. From the driver's side she crawled across to her friend and yanked and pulled awkwardly.

Amelia felt the resistance of the black vinyl seat against her cheek and she watched the metal shaft of the gear stick race up to meet her nose. "Ok, glad I didn't feel that," she thought.

Kimmy left Amelia crumpled in the car while she hurried around to hide the wheel chair between the concrete wall and the front of the neighboring vehicle. She quickly got into the driver's seat and closed the door. She adjusted her friend, secured her with the seat belt and reclined the seat so her head was supported. "Damn, girl you're just a bag of bones. You're a lot lighter than I thought you'd be."

Kimmy sat back in her seat and breathed a deep, cleansing and determined breath. Then she reached under the seat and brought out the little Ruger revolver. She checked the chamber; six rounds. "Thank you Margie," she whispered.

"Well I'm not going to hell for murder," said Kimmy as she pressed the revolver into Amelia's hand. "Can you feel that? That's the gun in your hand. Amelia did not blink, her hand didn't flinch. Kimmy removed the gun and leaned across Amelia's body to look her in the eyes. "We've talked about this. You can change your mind but if you do you'll be sitting here in a Volkswagen with my brains all over you until someone discovers us. Do you want to change your mind?"

Amelia could see herself in the rearview mirror; her disfigured face staring back. She blinked, hard, twice, "NO!"

"Do you want to take your own life with my help?" asked Kimmy, very slowly and with deliberate intention.

Amelia blinked one hard blink. "YES!"

"I know it's a long shot but if you can squeeze my hand when you're ready I'll finish it… this gun will blow a hole in the back of your head the size of a soft ball. I tried it on a watermelon once, so don't worry about being left here alive. I'm gonna close my eyes and I'm not opening them again – not ever. When I hear your cap explode – I'm turning the gun on myself." She pulled in another deep breath. "Ready?"

One blink.

Kimmy crawled across Amelia and straddled her legs. The tight compartment of the Volkswagen didn't leave much room between the two girls. "See you on the other side." She reached out a hand and wiped a tear from Amelia's cheek then slowly traced the scars on her disfigured face.

"Thanks for being a friend," Amelia thought with more affection than she had ever had for a friend. "I think you might have been someone I could depend on in life."

Kimmy braced her back against the dashboard as if expecting a kick from the small hand gun. She had fired the gun several times before. She knew it didn't kick; it was the kick of death she was bracing for. She wrapped Amelia's hand around the gun, turned her wrist so the barrel of the gun rested against her forehead. She took a deep breath and let it out slowly then closed her eyes. Kimmy waited for a moment, for a squeeze – when none came, she began the count; five, four, three, two –

"Do it, do it, do it," Amelia pleaded inwardly. Tears streamed down her scarred face.

There might have been a squeeze. There was definitely a blast. Kimmy felt the bits and pieces of Amelia's skull spatter her face. Without emotion and not more than a second delay, she turned the gun to her own forehead … and fired.

Chapter 11

When Esther's head struck the hard ceramic tile, a thump echoed through the quiet bank. The young teller leaned over the counter. "Ma'am, are you ok?"

Harlen sat reading his paper and waiting in his pickup. He checked his wristwatch and looked expectantly at the bank doors. An ambulance arrived. In the time it took to unload the gurney, Harlen had beaten the medics to the door. The bank manager's suit jacket was under Esther's head as a pillow. A well-dressed elderly woman knelt beside her and held her hand. The woman looked up at Harlen. "She just keeps calling for Millie. Do you know who that is?"

"Esther, honey, you ok?" he asked softly not knowing how to respond.

"She's gone, Harlen, she's gone." Esther didn't move at all when she spoke. Her voice was without emotion. She stared at Harlen. The paramedics took over.

***

It was quiet; not in an irreverent way, neither out of fear. It was an introspective silence. The line inched slowly forward and those at the front of the line faded then disappeared into a hazy cloud. The subtle lighting iridescently diffused the whiteness of the room giving the floors, walls and ceiling, if there were walls and a ceiling, an elusive quality. Amelia smelled fresh baked bread.

She *stood,* erect and beautiful; unscarred though she hadn't noticed. She was aware of her surroundings, of the compelling force that moved her forward to complete an undefined and predestined task; but she was not self-aware, not yet. Kimmy, in another line somewhere in the haze stood similarly composed as did an undeterminable number of others.

As Amelia moved gradually forward through the tranquil fog, a tangible destination began to materialize. She found herself standing before a large window. A white marble countertop separated Amelia from an unremarkable looking black woman. The woman wore no jewelry, she wore no makeup, she wore no expression. She wore white clothing.

The woman spoke a seemingly scripted dialogue "Amelia Specter you will be detained until it has been determined whether your suicide was justifiable. Please familiarize yourself with the rules of confinement and adhere to them for your safety." She handed Amelia a thin white book which contained thirty-seven pages of small print; no pictures. Behind the woman, silhouettes moved silently through the fog. "Violations will be viewed unfavorably on judgment day. An advisor will be assigned when you reach your destination. Please follow the blue path."

Again Amelia was compelled to move toward an unknown destination. When she turned the haze was gone; the building in which she stood was incomplete; missing the back portion and open to an outside world. Continuing, she saw birds and blue skies, trees and flowers. A blue foot bridge arched over a waterway. To the right of the bridge a red path entered a dark tunnel; to the left, a white path paralleled the waterway and meandered past park benches to a small dock. On a bench an elderly couple sat holding hands. They watched a ferry quietly paddle upstream with its passengers. The couple didn't appear to be saying goodbye to the ferry passengers, nor were they waiting for passage, there had been plenty of space available.

As Amelia moved involuntarily along the blue path toward the footbridge, she began to become aware of her motions. She saw her feet and realized she was walking. Her hands moved slowly to her face in search of the scars which were no longer present. As she crested the bridge, Amelia stopped walking and looked down at the blue path on which she stood. She noticed that her clothes were those she had worn on the day of her accident, blue jeans and a red sweatshirt embossed with the gold letters ISU. Her blond hair was pulled through the back of a tan ball cap.

She looked up the river to see where the ferry was heading. An azure sky was sparsely speckled with puffy white clouds; the grass along the river bank was green and lush. A fragrant bouquet of lilacs refreshed her senses and she smiled. Remembering the red path she turned to see what was up stream.

Steam crept low off of the water like a silently advancing enemy crawling along the surface. A gust of wind blew hot and wet. Where it continued out of the tunnel, the red path bled out onto a pier which protruded into the water way. Four men stood aboard a crudely constructed flat raft made of weathered scrap wood. There, at the raft's center, they clutched a metal pole at the rafts center which was topped by a cable threaded pulley. The cable was tethered to a towering sooted shaft which jutted up from the muddy bank.

The forlorn foursome included a young Hispanic man in saggy jeans and a Bulls jersey, his ball cap askew on his head; a middle aged professional sporting a tailored suit; a dingy older man whose denim jumpsuit badly needed washing. His bottom lip habitually sucked at his fuzzy grey mustache. Also aboard was a construction worker with a mustard hard hat, filthy Carhart overalls and a hoary beard so long that it quivered away from his neck in the hot wind. From the tunnel there emerged an abundantly tattooed woman with long dark unkempt hair. She wore a perpetual frown and an orange prison jumper. Polk County was printed in large white letters across her back. Methodically she crossed the pier to join the waiting men. Once aboard, the gate on the pier swung shut as the cable creaked the un-captained vessel into motion. The pulley system jerked the raft forward and dragged it reluctantly across the river. The passengers all steadied themselves at the centered mast to keep their balance.

Amelia glanced ahead to determine the boat's the destination and saw that a cable extended across the water way and into the narrow opening of an ox-bow lake. As the raft drew closer the water in the lake began to bubble, flames spat from the edges. Once inside the lake's perimeter the flames closed ranks, surrounding the raft. The passengers were no longer silent but fully cognizant and reactive. They backed away from the flames and huddled at the rear of the craft where the boiling water was now spitting stinging droplets at them.

The pulley slowed and finally halted while the flames licked at the perimeter of the vessel. Terrified, the passengers now flocked around the mast. The young man with the crooked ball cap lost his balance on the wet deck and grabbed the post. It burned his hand like a hot cast iron skillet. He quickly drew back in pain while hissing a Spanish expletive. The flames, now reaching over the deck of the boat, nipped at their feet.

Amelia could hear panicked screams. She also heard an unearthly moan that grew from the bowels of the hungry water into an outright deafening demonic roar. Like a wind whipped steaming kettle the air blew moist and steady; heat colored her face but she couldn't turn away.

One side of the raft began to rise from the water. Unable to keep her footing, the woman in the orange jumper slipped. She clawed frantically at the deck as she slid screaming toward the blazing water. Her finger tips caught in a crack and she was suspended from the craft; her legs dangled over the edge. Her bare feet began to burn and the fire crawled up her prison jumper. The men watched in horror and struggled for their own safety as she burned. The raft continued to incline. The well-dressed man whose slick shoes offered no traction grabbed the man in the ball cap and they both shot quickly past the still screaming woman and into the firey lake. The old man went next, his face scraped on the floor of the boat so that the flesh of it was melted away before he hit the boiling and burning water. The bearded construction worker had wrapped his hands in his overall sleeves and was clinging to the metal mast which now stuck out at a thirty degree angle over the water. The woman's charred body broke off at the finger tips and was swallowed by the lake. The bearded man's shoes began to melt. His beard caught fire. He let loose of the mast and plunged into the inferno.

Amelia smelled a combination of burnt flesh and the sulfuric, acrid odor of brimstone. Instantaneously, columns of flames shot high into the smoky sky before they were swallowed with a shrill cry by the lake which fed them.

Amelia was drenched in sweat. She felt nauseous as she stepped off of the bridge and onto a train station platform. She boarded the waiting car and took a seat. A few others joined her at lengthy intervals; all of them sweating, red faced and stunned. No one spoke as the train jerked away from the platform.

Chapter 12

A plume of vapor hissed into the crisp air as one of the last ever, newly constructed, British Railway steam locomotives pulled away from Boone's Scenic Valley Railroad Station. Kimmy's friends and family had their own personal car at the rear of the train. Two poster boards were full of photographs, mostly of Kimmy and her friends. Jimmy could only find four photos at home of Kimmy; two were taken when she was just a toddler, another was a strip photo of Jimmy and Kimmy which was taken at a black and white photo booth in the mall. They were ten and fifteen years old, acting silly as kids do in a photo booth. The other was the only family picture that ever existed. Kimmy was a baby, six or eight months old, propped on her mother's hip. Her mom wore heavy blue eye shadow and a big black wig in the bouffant style of the day. She had on a tight powder blue sweater that showed off her full chest and a red checked mini skirt. In her free hand she happily displayed her beverage of choice; Old Milwaukee. Her dad, with blue jeans and a plain white tee shirt, a pack of Camel's in his sleeve and one dangling from his lips stood with his family; he didn't smile. Jimmy, on the opposite side of mom, was six years old. He sported orange and brown checked bell bottoms also with a plain white tee shirt. His eyes were crossed; he had pulled his lips wide with his fingers and stuck out his tongue -- A not so Norman Rockwell looking picture.

A compilation of Kimmy's favorite music played on a cassette player to Margie's right. To her left sat a bundle of red roses. Also on the bench were three similarly gothic attired friends; Jo Jo, Spoof and Trash. The only male of the motley gaggle, Trash wore a wrinkled black duster that draped just above his high top black Converse. Atop his jet black curly mullet perched a novelty fedora adorned by a single red and ragged feather tucked into the hat band. The girls were also cloaked in black garb from head to toe. Jo Jo and Spoof wore pale foundation, heavy black eye liner and grey lipstick. A small silver cross hung from a delicate hoop which pierced Spoof's left nostril. Margie's attire was similar with the exception of three black inked tear drops which cascaded down her left cheek; she wore no makeup at all. Together they solemnly sat with their backs to the passing scenery.

Jimmy and his father, quietly seated opposite the divergent crew, listened to the four share antics of their lost friend. Kimmy's small family did not reciprocate. When the train turned up the banks of the Des Moines River, Margie fast forwarded the cassette - Cleansed by Fire, Alice Cooper.

"I don't know but I've been told the streets of hell are paved with gold – Crazy, crazy." The song played on. As the last stanza played "You lose and I win, you couldn't suck me in. It's over, you have no power. You're lost and I'm found and I'm heaven bound. Go back to where you belong, to where you fell. Go to hell." When a church bell chimed on the cassette Margie pushed open the window and emptied the pine box of ashes into the chilly winter wind. She tossed the box after it.

Out the window Margie shouted, "Just like you wanted Kimmy, down to the letter. You raise some hell in heaven for me girl. I'll see ya when I get there."

With tear filled eyes, Margie distributed flowers. She stood silently at the window, kissed her rose and tossed it out. The three friends followed the solemn gesture. Jimmy pulled a single petal from the rose before he let his go. Kimmy's father looked uncomfortable with the ritual but followed suit.

When the hour long ride ended the train lurched to a halt. Without a word or a tear Kimmy's father climbed up into the cab of his Kenworth and headed off to deliver a load of Carnation baby formula to a warehouse in Peoria. Jimmy stood alone and watched him go. His isolation was briefly interrupted as Margie laid a tender hand on his shoulder and delivered a sad and gentle kiss to his cheek. She handed him back his family photos.

***

The packed funeral home needed to open two additional rooms of seating to accommodate the crowd of mourners at Amelia's funeral. Delivery vans waited in a convoy to bring sprays and blankets, vases and plants. The entire ISU swim team sat together, each holding a single rose.

It was a Presbyterian funeral, part eulogy, part sermon; full of biblical verse and Amens. A beautiful girl, a near replica of a Barbie doll, stood before the gathering.

"Aunt Esther and Uncle Harlen have an old wooden swing that hangs from a really old oak tree in the back yard. Millie was swinging on it the last time I saw her, about a week before her accident. When we were kids we used to push each other and pretend we were flying. Whoever had the seat was the pilot and got to pick the destination. I always wanted to fly to all of the exotic tourist spots like Hawaii or Disney. Millie always wanted to go to the moon. She'd vary it by taking us past different planets or constellations but her final destination was the same. My wish for her is that she got to visit the moon on her trip to heaven and that she was able to look down on us. She'd say, "Barbie," her voice caught in her throat and tears welled in her eyes, "take that vacation to Hawaii because life is too short." She had more to say and stood for a long moment, looked to the ceiling and tried to compose herself. Finally she said in a broken and tear filled voice "love ya 'scuzzin.' " Since they were little girls they affectionately had referred to each other as the scuzzy cousin. She returned to her seat where her mother wrapped her in her arms. They hugged and sobbed while the minister invited friends to pass the casket to pay their final respects.

The autonomic response that allows a person to function; to breathe in and out, to swallow, to blink and to sit upright, were all that existed in Esther. Her lungs expelled air, her spine supported her and her broken heart continued to beat. But her red and swollen eyes held no more tears and her face no apparent expression. Beside her, Harlen sat in a new suit, his only suit. With his shoulders slumped and head bowed, tears dripped from the end of his nose onto folded hands. He did not look in the direction of any of the guests that walked before him.

A single 8x10 framed photograph of Amelia, beautiful and smiling while sitting in the tree swing, sat atop the casket. As the members of the swim team passed, each laid a rose by the photo. Alex William Garreth discretely took a single petal from the flower before he left his rose.

***

Jimmy placed the vase with six red roses next to Hope's bedside. He pulled a chair up next to the little girl's bed and collapsed into it. Overcome with grief, he sobbed into his tobacco stained hands. After a long while he looked up to the ceiling, with moist and bloodshot eyes and a tear soaked face he whispered, "Oh kiddo, I will miss you so much."

Outside of the hospital room stood the nurse sporting a Garfield the cat neck-scarf. She remembered Jimmy from his previous visit and she knew, the whole country knew, about his sister's death. Just inside the doorway, but out of Jimmy's sight, she silently folded her arms and rested her head against the wall. Here, she also cried. She cried for his pain and for the little girl, Hope. She cried for the suffering and grieving people she dealt with every day. She cried for her own loneliness and emotional exhaustion. Then she wiped her tears and slipped out of the room unseen.

Chapter 13

"Code blue 2121, code blue 2121" was quietly announced.
Two nurses ran down the hall and into room 2121. Dirk Cooper lay in
a growing pool of blood, a double edged shaving blade in his hand and
his prosthetic leg lodged foot side up in the toilet bowl. The hospital
orderly who had discovered him held a drenched bloody towel to
Dirk's throat.

Several stitches and several liters of blood later, Dirk lay
sedated in the critical care unit. "Let's transfer him to ward B and get a
psychological profile. I want him heavily sedated for the next week,"
said the doctor.

Dirk's vacant and glazed eyes stared in the direction of the
orderly who cleaned up the gory gauze 4x4's and mopped the blood
spattered floor. Only a few feet from Dirk's bed the orderly

momentarily halted his duties and stared eye to eye with the patient. Then Evron James Brown smiled slightly and went back to his task.

***

The train's whistle blew as it came to a stop south of the Harger Blish office building; long since deserted, the cornerstone said 1910. Amelia knew those tracks to be abandoned yet she was stepping off of a passenger train. Without a word, the porter motioned the passengers to the dilapidated old building. The windows and doors on the first floor were boarded up. The exposed upper level windows were mostly shattered. It was dark. When the handful of refugees reached what had been the main entrance to the building, a door opened and soft white light spilled out onto the side walk.

"Welcome to the Harger Blish, for your safety, please adhere strictly to the rules outlined in your post life manual and the rules posted throughout the building. Enjoy your provisional amnesty," said the doorman.

The interior of the building did not at all resemble the office space which had been the buildings most recent use, rather it looked and felt like a turn of the century hotel with high ceilings, thick hand dyed wool carpet and walnut wainscoting that skirted plaster stucco walls. There was a registration desk, also of polished walnut, where a female clerk sat reading a paperback novel. Behind her on the wall hung several large black and white photos of Des Moines and of the Harger Blish building in its early days.

Amelia wanted to more closely examine the pictures but she and the others were ushered into an auditorium. On the stage stood a podium; behind it, a small man wearing a brown wool suite, a bolo and wire rimmed glasses. She looked around in stunned amazement. The room was nearly half full; about fifty people sat bewildered and mesmerized before the small man on the stage. Briefly she scanned the room for Kimmy, before being urged by the usher to sit.

The door to the auditorium shut with a heavy thud and the lights over the audience dimmed. "Welcome to the Harger Blish," the small man now illuminated by a spotlight announced. "This building is listed on the national historic registry; with spiritual influence upon committee members, it should remain so, providing a sanctuary for lingering souls and for those not yet judged. Similar sites are located around the globe. The comfortable accommodations you see are only apparitions, as are you. This structure will appear to living human eyes exactly as they have left it and we will occupy it for as long as it stands. Please be comfortable here but adhere strictly to the rules.

He continued, "Upon your death you were given either passage to heaven or a stay of judgment. For those of you who have been granted passage we thank you for your benevolence and wish you a good journey at your leisure. However, we urge you to make peace and pay the ferryman without undo haste. Bliss and rejuvenation await you on the other side."

"Each of you came to us today via a registration port nearest your place of death. At the time of death there are four possible judgments."

"The first and the least desirable is that you are guilty of sins against God and humanity without remittance. The sentence is a one way trip into the firey lake of hell followed by an eternity of suffering."

"The second is guilty to a lesser degree. Your sins were vast, malicious and intentional however the sum of the deeds of your life were absent of malice. For this, purgatory holds permanent servitude."

"The third judgment is guilty with guarded cause. You waged a great sin resulting in or intending for the greater good of others and the sum of the deeds of your life have been noble. If you are found to be in this category, your stay in purgatory will be temporary. Servitude will be required so that you may atone for your sins but you will eventually be granted passage to heaven when sufficient time has passed."

"The final course of action is for those of you who have lived a life with primarily compassionate and selfless behavior. The sum of your life's actions far outweigh any minor transgression. You have admittance to heaven at your leisure."

"Purgatory servitude can take many forms including the duties that I and every soul on staff here carry out. Some purgatories serve to provide for the desires of individuals granted heavenly status or those awaiting judgment, others are given undistinguishable identities and work in undesirable earthbound positions. They are provided with modest dwellings and minimal furnishings. Contact with people is only as absolutely necessary for duty and survival. Social contact is forbidden. They are the hermits of human society. Any money earned by purgatories pays for their housing, for the influence of preservation societies and for the stipend to waiting souls. Remaining funds are used for anonymous charitable contributions."

"When your judgment has been passed your advisor will contact you and explain in detail the terms and conditions of your sentence. Violations of your sentence, like violations of our rules, will not be looked upon favorably and may result in severe consequences." The little man continued his speech for a lengthy period. He outlined each chapter in the Post Life Manual.

Chapter One: Welcome to Purgatory

Chapter Two: The Advisor – A mentor for the Afterlife

Chapter Three: Cellular Restructuring - When and How to Leave the
Building
Chapter Four: Patching Holes – Indistinct Visits to Loved Ones
Chapter Five: Angels and Demons – The Natural Forces of Pure Good
and Evil
Chapter Six: Death after Death – The Destruction of a Soul
Chapter Seven: Judgment Day

"It is highly important that you read and understand your
manual thoroughly. This concludes your orientation. Please report to
the registration desk for your room assignments." The squeaky little
man in the brown suit, bolo and wire rimmed glasses turned and
vanished into the darkness of the stage before the lights in the
auditorium rose.

In an orderly and patient manner the crowd filtered out. Amelia
spotted Kimmy in the lobby. She was almost directly in front of
Kimmy when she was finally recognized.

"Oh my God!" Kimmy exclaimed as she threw her arms
around Amelia's neck and hugged her enthusiastically. She pulled
back and examined her friend with a wide smile and hugged her again.
"You are beautiful! I can't believe it. Holy shit, look at you!" Amelia
laughed; embarrassed by the compliment and absurdly aware of the
irony in Kimmy's statement. Kimmy clasped a hand to her mouth

then looked up to the ceiling and sheepishly apologized to "the big guy".

The girls quietly smiled at each other with restrained delight as they crept toward the registration desk with a crowd that was oblivious to their aberrant excitement. The elderly woman at the registration desk addressed them without expression. "Amelia Specter and Kimberly Shobek you were deceased in union would you like a joint room?"

"Yes please," Kimmy blurted. "Is that ok?"

"Absolutely," said Amelia. "I'd be so lonely without your one-sided conversation to keep me company."

The clerk handed each of them a small package and gave them their room number.

The room was a typical looking hotel room, two beds, night stand, reading light; they sat opposite each other on their beds. Kimmy rifled through the bureau drawers. "No Bible, no TV." She looked at the phone. Bewildered she said, "Who would we call?"

Amelia went through the package given to her at the front desk. There was a paperback novel – To Kill A Mocking Bird, a hair brush, scissors, nail trimmers, three emery boards and twenty individual dollar bills. She held up the scissors and nail trimmers and looked quizzically at Kimmy.

Kimmy formed circles with both of her hands and placed them over her eyes. She said in a nasally voice, "Hair and nails grow rapidly on the recently deceased please groom yourself as necessary. Violations of our rules will not be looked upon favorably and may result in severe consequences."

Amelia laughed but her smile quickly faded to a look of incomprehension. "I can't believe we're dead and I'm just sitting here talking to you like nothing ever happened. I'm not sure what I expected but *this* was not it." She stood and went to the window, pulled back the curtain and looked to her amazement at a city bustling with morning traffic; business as usual. Kimmy picked up the handbook and settled back on her pillow to read. The room was silent for a long while until she heard the sound of the shower. Amelia shut the bathroom door and examined her unscarred, youthful face in the mirror, until eventually it fogged over from the steam.

Chapter 14

Out of the fog …Thud thump, thud thump, thud thump. Backlit
by glowing street lights, Dirk appeared ghoulish as he approached the
waiting car. His buddy; a large, unkempt man, smelling of alcohol and
cheap cigarettes stood waiting, puffing away at a Lucky Strike under
the awning of Mercy hospital's main entrance. Dirk opened the back
door and tossed his crutches onto the seat. He had carried them out at
his side like a rifle case. Dirk was intent on regaining his strength and
his dignity; crutches were not an option. Anyone who knew Dirk
Cooper also knew his flagrant idiosyncrasies. He had no tolerance for
weakness or infirmity, which is why he had not one visitor in the six
weeks he'd been hospitalized. Dirk never visited a friend in the
hospital, disliked cemeteries and in general just didn't want anything
to do with disease or death.

He explained this to his scruffy pal over a jack and coke at the smoke filled tavern, "When I was little my grandmother died of emphysema – smoked like a chimney right up to the end." Dirk crushed out his cigarette butt in the overflowing ash tray in front of him. "That woman was in and out of the hospital all of the time. When we'd visit, Mom used to say, 'Don't breathe too deep in this place, you'll catch the diseases of the sick people.' "

His friend watched the silent Monday night football game on the TV over the bar; Dirk continued talking into his drink. "When grandma died I sat in the car for the funeral. Mom didn't want me to look at her in the casket; said it would give me nightmares. But when we got to the cemetery and they lowered that box in the ground I kept thinking grandma wasn't dead yet. I was sure they were putting her in there kicking and screaming. I thought I could *hear* her kicking and screaming. You know the imagination of a ten year old! I told mom what I thought and she laughed at me – said granny was dead but she'd sure enough come back to haunt me if I wasn't good. Mom could tell that creeped me out and she used it on me all the time. If a light bulb flickered she'd say, "Granny's watchin." Once I beat up the neighbor kid, kicked his butt for taking my sister's school books. I left him crying in a crumpled heap while other kids stood and laughed. Riding my bike home I turned back to look at the circle of kids and hit a phone poll; lost two teeth. Mom said granny ran me into that poll for being bad."

A heavy cloud of cigarette smoke consumed the air, glasses and bottles knocked on tabletops and random chatter filled the bar. Dirk took in the static for a moment before he continued, "Do you think it's true? Ya think dead people stick around to punish others? Ya think maybe some accidents aren't accidents and the people who died are just pissed off?" He didn't expect an answer and his friend wasn't listening.

He drank his rum and coke and thought back to the fight, his dead opponent, the crash, the hospital and Evron snickering at his bedside. He suddenly and startlingly recalled a dream-like experience with unearthly qualities: an endless line of people shrouded in fog, Evron walking next to him, a violent tug and the sensation of falling back into his body. Dirk put his drink down unfinished, stood and limped from the bar without saying a word.

***

Holding a steaming cup of coffee Dirk thought to himself, "How do I know him?" He had just delivered a load of Styrofoam coffee cups, Dixie stir sticks, paper napkins and paper plates to Pop's Coffee Shop. Paper products were light, easy for him to handle as he continued to learn to balance on the prosthetic pedestal. While he

89

waited for the owner's signature he sipped his coffee and took in his surroundings.

An Asian man in the corner sat sipping a cup and reading the Des Moines Register. "How do I know him?" Dirk restated this time out loud. From behind the counter Max Long, the owner, said, "Probably saw him last week. The guy's in here practically every night." He signed the bill and handed it to Dirk.

"Na, it's from somewhere else, I just can't place it." He looked perplexed and stared blatantly at the patron who sat sipping his coffee and reading. Dirk shook his head to clear the thought. "See ya next week Max." He left.

***

At home he lay in bed staring at the ceiling; searching his thoughts for the vexing image of the man at the coffee shop. Eventually Dirk drifted into a fitful sleep, one wrought with disturbing visions and memories.

He was nine years old, home alone shortly after his grandmother's funeral. Flipping through a photo album, he came across a picture of his grandmother taken just before her death. She wore a floral print house dress with clunky black shoes and thick tan support hose. She looked reproachfully over her shoulder at the photographer while she washed dishes at the sink. Nine year old Dirk stood waist high looking up at her, a dish towel dangled from his small hands.

As he studied the photo it began to come to life in his hands. Nothing in the picture moved accept the old woman's face. She said, "Why aren't you at my funeral boy? Don't you love your old granny? I practically raised you, gave every penny I could to keep you and your momma from starving and this is the thanks I get? You disrespect me by not even showing up to my funeral. I'll show you boy, you'll be sorry you treated me this way. I'll get you boy, you'll be sorry!"

Dirk tossed in his bed and the dream took new form. He was eleven, riding his bike home from school. He turned to look over his shoulder at two very attractive teenaged girls and rode his bike into a parked car. Except for his ego, he wasn't hurt much. However, the fender of his bike was bent into the front tire which was now flat. When the kitchen screen door whapped his mother spun around. "What the hell happened to you?" She snapped. The tear in his jeans exposed an oozing red scrape on his knee.

"I wrecked my bike," he said as if it had been a stupid question.

His mother smirked and crossed her arms. "You must have done something to piss grandma off. You mess up she'll put you in line. You better watch your step and do what's right son."

Again the dream morphed. Dirk saw himself as an adult, standing in his mother's bathroom. His prosthetic leg balanced precariously on the fingertips of his left hand. He steadied himself at the porcelain sink bowl while teetering on his remaining good leg and watched the blood slowly dripped from the freshly dismembered stump of his right leg. He heard, "You better watch your step or you'll be sorry." His grandmother's face stared back at him in the vanity mirror.

Dirk tossed, sweat drenched his bed, as he tried in wakeless vain to push away the dreams. Now he was in a bright light at the end of a dark tunnel. He kept walking, unable to stop. He was met simultaneously by another figure that was also approaching from the darkness. The two joined in the light. Evron and Dirk exchanged a bewildered look and continued moving involuntarily toward their destination. They stood, each in their own lines. The subtle lighting iridescently diffused the whiteness of the room giving the floors, walls and ceiling –if there were walls and a ceiling, an intangible quality. He smelled fresh baked bread. The line inched slowly forward and those at the front of the line faded then disappeared into a hazy cloud.

Dirk stood on two legs. Evron appeared clean and unscathed. His name was softly announced: Evron James Brown.

Dirk felt a violent backward jolt. The line parted. One man, one single Asian man, the man from the coffee shop turned to watch him fall back, fall through the darkening tunnel away from the light.

Breathing heavily and ensnared by sweat drenched bed sheets he jerked himself awake. Frustrated by his subconscious fear he ripped back the sheet and jumped to his feet - to his foot - he forgot. He fell to the floor with a thud.

Chapter 15

When Amelia re-entered the room her damp hair was tucked under a fluffy white terrycloth towel which matched her bathrobe. Kimmy thought Amelia looked angelic, like she deserved to be in heaven. For the first time Kimmy questioned her own fate. She sat cross legged in the oversized arm-chair, the open handbook in her lap.

She shook off the thought and explained to Amelia what she had just read. "We can eat but we don't require food. We can drink but we won't get drunk. We probably don't sweat either but a shower sure does sound good. I'm gonna get one." She tossed Amelia the book as she stood and walked to the bathroom. After a minute she leaned out of the bathroom door, her naked torso hidden by the door frame. "I bet if we shit, it doesn't stink," she said with a grin. She slapped the door frame as if she amused herself and disappeared into the bathroom.

Amelia was glad to have her friend with her. Kimmy's lighthearted commentary took some of the weight off the predicament. It was just as welcome in death as it had grown to be in the hospital. Amelia initially thought their pairing was the ultimate cruel fate; two personalities could not have been more opposite. But Kimmy's unrestricted innocence and playfulness quickly won her over. Amelia thought about how Kimmy bounced on her bed and touched her scarred face like a curious toddler. Her own mother hadn't the courage to touch the disfigurement. Her antics were the only thing that Amelia looked forward to at the end and for that little bit of joy, Amelia was eternally grateful. Certainly such a vulnerable, kind and candid person would be admitted to heaven she thought.

But how would she be judged when she had been so judgmental. In an introspective purgatory, Amelia now thought herself to be self-absorbed and close-minded. She questioned her own fate. Amelia thought about Alex Garreth. Why hadn't she just confronted him instead of assuming the worst and labeling him a fraud? Everyone else seemed to really like him but she had refused to give him a chance. She had labeled Kimmy a freak initially and, had she legs that worked, she would have walked out of the room, never giving Kimmy a second chance. How many others had she labeled and slammed the door on, she wondered.

Kimmy stepped out of the bathroom pulling on the black t-shirt she had arrived in; her wet ponytail dampened her back. "Let's check this place out," she said.

Large double doors slowly squeaked open to reveal an empty ball room, grand and elaborate. A heavy crystal chandelier hung from the muraled ceiling. Candles burned on the elegant tables that ringed the beautiful high glossed wooden dance floor. Tall trellises of flowers cascaded with color, but no music played. "This place is amazing," said Amelia.

"So elegant and so wasted; why go to such trouble for dead people?" Kimmy remarked. "Especially ones stuck in limbo. You'd think this would be a hotel for the rich and famous."

"Or the righteous and benevolent," said Amelia.

"Humor – wow that's something new," Kimmy smirked.

Amelia smelled food and heard the clinking of dishes being shuffled. She headed down a hallway in search of the noise when she heard…

"PSST."

Kimmy was standing under an exit sign leading to a side door. She nodded toward the door. Amelia took one step then hesitated. Kimmy nodded more vigorously. Amelia joined her. They stopped short at the door and looked at each other mustering the courage to face what they would find on the outside. Amelia took Kimmy's hand and in unison they took a deep breath. When Kimmy reached for the door handle they were enormously startled by a booming voice from behind.

"You ought not to go out into the sunlight. Don't want you fading away from us so soon." A large black man was standing not two feet from them.

"Name is Evron Brown… Evron James Brown," he stated in a voice that demanded respect. "You cannot be seen in the sunlight. If ever you are caught in the sunlight your form will fade away. It will be retrieved and rejuvenated in your designated room after much time has passed… I suggest you read the book."

He wore a uniform vest similar to the clerk's. Kimmy held a look of recognition and bewilderment.

As they walked back to their room Kimmy thought to herself, "How do I know him?"

Chapter 16

Back in their room Amelia sprawled flat on her bed, engrossed in *the book.*

Chapter Four: Patching holes – Indistinct Visits.

You are welcome and encouraged to visit unobtrusively anyone from your past. This is a multipurpose voyage which allows you not only to comfort your soul, but also to indiscreetly console grieving loved ones on a subconscious level; thereby patching holes of sorrow that would hinder your happiness in heaven.

Be mindful. This journey will be exhausting. You will tire quickly and will require much time for recuperation.

To begin this journey, lie back in a comfortable position. Think of a place in life when you were truly happy and recreate that place. Think only of that place until you reach your destination. Once you have been transported to your chosen destination simply think of a person and you will be in their presence.

Amelia did not finish the chapter. She looked over at Kimmy to tell her what she had just read but Kimmy was comatose. Mouth agape and snoring, the open book bridged her cheek to the pillow.

Amelia closed her book. She pressed the wrinkles from her shirt, adjusted her hair and slowly lay back on her pillow. She took a deep breath and held it a moment, then, trembling with fear and anticipation she slowly exhaled. With her fingers laced and resting across her stomach she continued to breath deep and exhale slowly. After a few breaths the index finger of her right hand began to twitch. The twitch spread to the other fingers; her hands began to jerk. As the spasms migrated to her feet, arms and legs, a smile slowly stretched across her face. As the smile developed the twitching slowed. She lay quietly, peacefully, content.

Kimmy stirred on the adjacent bed. She arched her back and stretched her fingers toward the headboard. The book fell to the floor. When she reached to retrieve it she saw that Amelia was asleep. Kimmy went to the sink and splashed water on her face. She examined herself in the mirror, repositioned her disheveled hair and scratched a speck on her cheek with her finger nail. Noticing that her nails were longer, she went back to her bed side dresser to get the file and brush. As she turned she bumped the dresser hard almost knocking over the lamp, she caught it before it fell. Despite the ruckus, Amelia did not stir.

In the bathroom, Kimmy sat on the toilet lid and clipped her nails into a waste basket. She filed them then stood to examine herself once more in the mirror. Her hair was longer she observed as she ran her fingers through it. She brushed it straight. When satisfied she peaked around the corner to see if Amelia was still sleeping. Certain that she was, Kimmy turned to leave and fell over a box that had been placed outside their door. She made a terrible racket but still Amelia slept. Kimmy shook her head in amazement then picked up the large, now crumpled box and returned to her bed.

Inside the box were two smaller boxes addressed one to each of them. In her box she found a loose knit brown sweater, a brown knit stocking cap and matching mittens. She opened the closet and placed her box beneath a brown wool winter coat, next to black winter boots. She pulled off her t-shirt and pulled on the sweater. Again glancing at Amelia, she left the room, shutting the door quietly behind her.

There were people again in the main hall. The dining room was full. Kimmy wasn't hungry. The book had said she wouldn't be.

Eating was purely for recreation; "I guess you don't need to nourish a corpse," she had quipped earlier to her friend.

The most incredible smells came from the kitchen. Compulsively, she went in search of the smell. At the door to the kitchen she paused. A whisk beat rapidly against a metal bowl. When the whipping sound stopped she heard a female voice softly signing "Oh Millie, Oh Billie... Criminally insane... Oh Millie, Oh Billie..." She slowly pushed through the galley doors. "I've been waiting for you," said a distantly familiar female voice.

Pulses of light mixed with childhood memories flashed through her mind. Dizzily, Kimmy's world spun and she grabbed desperately at the white ceramic tiles of the kitchen wall for support as she slid to the floor.

***

Pulses of light popped off images like black and white still photos. A pastoral hillside dotted with oaks and maples, a distant dirt road disappearing into parallel rows of tall corn. A bi-colored border collie smiled around a slobbery tennis ball. In another snapshot a fair haired woman in knit pants and a floral button down smock sat on a clapboard porch hulling peas. The same woman stood in sloppy mud boots smiling widely at a new born calf struggling to stand. A man doffing a Pioneer Seed Corn cap sat atop a John Deer tractor with a little pig-tailed girl at the wheel on his lap. The same man pushed the same widely grinning little girl on a tire swing which was tied to an old and very thick maple tree. A black and white dog sat next to a maple tree. The woman leaned against the maple tree. The little girl sat beneath the maple tree reading a book.

This image, the little girl under the maple tree, slowly took color and life as the little girl faded away. The leaves were an early autumn mix of green and gold, the sky was turquoise spattered with wispy white clouds. Birds chirped. A light breeze stirred the air which was imbued with the scent of fresh baked bread. Amelia realized that she had materialized, that she was home.

The tree was a place where she played as a child, studied and sometimes napped or ate her meals. It was where she dreamed of how her life would be. She was happy there. Then she thought of why she was there. She was on a journey to patch the holes she had left in life. Immediate on her list was to see that her mother and father were comforted and adjusting. She knew that she would find them grieving and was prepared for this. She hoped that they would feel her on some level and would be quieted by her presence but she also knew this was not likely. Amelia leaned against the tree, closed her eyes and concentrated on her mother's face.

The sounds of the chirping birds subsided. She brought into her mind the image of her mother; Thanksgiving when her mother had stumbled over the dog and dropped a full gravy boat. It landed upside down on the dog's head and stuck. The dog pawed it and it fell to the floor. Cookie stuffed her nose deep into the bowl and pushed it across the floor licking at the gravy until she ran it into a wall and shoved the dish hard onto her nose. When Cookie backed away from the wall, the gravy boat was stuck on her nose. Doing circles with her head in the air she kept licking the dish. Esther was brought to laughing tears. As the image narrowed to just her mother's face, the face morphed from laughter to sobbing. The once sparkling eyes were suddenly swollen and red. As more of the picture developed, shaking shoulders accompanied feverish sobs instead of joyful laughter. Finally, Amelia was in the presence of her mother; looking down on her in a hospital bed. Esther was alone in the room; tethered to her bed by a heart monitor, an IV and a nasal cannula.

***

She sobbed hard and with gasping breaths as her mother rocked her in her arms. "It's ok child," Kimmy's mother said softly. "We all meet again sometime in this world or the other. But I can't talk with you right now. I'm serving my time and I'll cook here until my time is served. Then child, I will meet you in heaven." She kissed Kimmy's forehead and returned to her whisk and bowl.

Kimmy lay fetaly immobilized, unsure that her emotionally traumatized body would support her. After what seemed a long time had passed she regained her composure enough to stand. Weak and bewildered, she backed slowly through the galley doors while watching her mother diligently complete her chores. This woman, whom she had resented for leaving her motherless; who should have kissed her bumps and bruises and protected her from life's misfortunes, was here and someday soon, in death, her mother would comfort her as a mother should.

She wiped her tears on her sleeve and thought of Amelia. She had to wake her friend to tell her that she had met her mother. If her mother hadn't gone to hell for all *she* had done then surely, she thought, they would also be spared.

She burst into the room and stopped short at what she saw. Amelia lay just as she did when Kimmy had left. Her fingers laced across her chest she looked like she had been laid out for a funeral.

"Amelia," she said softly… no response. She said it a little louder and tapped her gently on the shoulder. No response. With wide and frightened eyes she shouted "Amelia!" She shook her friend forcefully. Kimmy had shaken her so hard that Amelia's head slipped from the pillow, she lay at an angle on the bed her fingers still laced.

Kimmy raced from the room down the hall to the front desk. Other guests stared in the direction of the commotion. Just as she reached the front desk a voice from behind her said "can I help you." Kimmy wheeled around; panic on her face. The woman wore the uniform of the hotel.

"My friend," she said, "she's....not, not moving. There's something wrong can you send someone – a doctor or someone?" The woman took a step toward Kimmy and motioned formally for Kimmy to lead the way. Feeling at the same time both conspicuous and frantic, she took a deep breath to calm herself and walked quickly back to her room. The door was still open – still Amelia had not moved. The woman went to her. She picked up her head and gently straightened her on the bed. She repositioned the pillow. Then she looked at the handbook at the foot of Amelia's bed. She turned stiffly to Kimmy. Then she looked at the handbook on Kimmy's bedside table. When the woman placed the book purposefully in Kimmy's hand she said "You haven't read the handbook have you?" Kimmy looked puzzled.

"Amelia is just fine," the woman opened the book to a chapter titled Patching Holes. "Read it" she said and left the room.

Kimmy felt a little foolish but she was also a little irked by the woman's chastising behavior. She crawled up to the head board propped some pillows then wiggled into them. She opened the book and leafed through a few pages. With a big sigh she said out loud "I wonder if there is an audio version of this."

You are welcome and encouraged to visit unobtrusively anyone from your past.

"Blah, Blah, Blah, Blah"

Be mindful. The journey will be exhausting. You will tire quickly and will require much time for recuperation.

To begin this journey,…

Kimmy looked over at Amelia and saw that her expression had changed. She had a painful grimace on her face as if she wanted to look away but couldn't.

***

Amelia knew she had caused the pain her mother now felt, the guilt was tremendous. She expected her mother to be grieving but she didn't expect it to have affected her in such a way that she needed to be hospitalized. The oxygen monitor beeped. A nurse entered the room and pushed a sedative into the IV. She took Esther's pulse and waited for the sedative to work before she caringly touched Esther's cheek, grimaced sympathetically and left the room. Her mother slept now with deep breaths. Amelia wanted to be closer – to touch her mother and try to comfort her. Simply wishing it made it happen. She lowered herself from the ceiling where she had hovered. She was uncertain about maneuvering in this form since she hadn't read that far. She was shocked at how fluid she felt. No sudden movements; she just floated where she willed herself to go. When she was at her mother's bedside, she tried to put her hand on the bed rails but it passed right through. This startled her just a little then she realized that her feet were gone. She was partially in the floor and although it made no physiological difference, the look of it disturbed her. She adjusted so that she was hovering slightly above the floor. Her hands stretched out in front of her as if to touch her mother's cheek but careful not to, Amelia said, "It's me Mom, Millie. I'm ok Mom. You and Dad will get through this. It will take you some time but you'll see that it was for the best. I couldn't bear the thought of the sacrifices you would have made on my behalf. You would have never been able to enjoy your life taking care of me. I would have never been able to enjoy my life knowing the burden I was to you. Mom I'm so sorry I've done this to you, but I did it *for* you."

The door behind her opened and her father walked into the room with coffee in his hand. He went straight to the bedside and right through Amelia. She gasped and moved backward as quickly as she could. Although she felt shaken, violated and panicked, her father hadn't noticed a thing. Amelia spun around to check herself for holes then regained her composer. Harlen had moved to the recliner by the window. He turned his face to the darkened Des Moines skyline. It was a view that Amelia had stared at for hours from just a few floors up. Amelia floated near the window to observe her father's face. His eyes were closed tightly, his lips pursed to hold in the sound of his crying, tears streamed down his face. In all of her life, she had never seen him cry. She bent down to her knees still hovering above the floor. Placing her hands barely above his knees she looked up into his grief-stricken face and said, "Oh Daddy, I'm so sorry. What have I done to you? Please forgive me for causing you this pain, I only meant to help."

An orderly entered.

"Mr. Specter."

Her father stood and Amelia somersaulted backward trying to avoid another intrusion.

"You have some visitors, would you like me to show them in?"

He wiped his eyes with the heels of his hands and silently nodded. Aunts and uncles and cousins, eight of them, filed into the small room. Amelia went for the ceiling to avoid contact. Feeling trapped, she hastily made for the door, crawling as if she needed to hold onto the ceiling to keep from falling. At the door she took a deep breath, gathering courage to pass through the solid and then she went out into the hall.

Looking back at the closed door, she descended to the floor, turned around and looked straight into the face of Evron James Brown.

Startled, she flew straight back to the ceiling and crouched on it like a cat holding tight to a tree branch.

Evron turned and look up at Amelia. "Be careful you do not stay too long on your first journey. The recovery is long." When he walked away, an orderly bumped him. "Excuse me," he said.

"Evron Brown was here *in body*. How could that be?" she thought. Then she thought of the door at the hotel where she had first met Mr. Brown. "Don't go out into the sunlight, we wouldn't want you fading away from us so soon," he had said to them.

Suddenly she felt herself falling backward. She remembered the book … to return to the Harger Blish you need only to think of it.

Her body jumped as she fell into it. She opened her eyes and turned her head. Kimmy lay on the bed, her intertwined fingers twitching. Amelia tried to focus on her friend but her eyes were heavy. She slept.

Chapter 17

The man at the coffee shop, the man in his dream tormented him. The main library was downtown near Mercy hospital. He stopped before going to therapy. Whirling through a real of micro fiche, he searched for September 28th, 1988, the day after his accident. "Dukakis Assailed Bush for Picking Dan Quayle as Running Mate" was the headline in the Des Moines Register. Local Man Looses Leg When Bike and Deer Collide was a byline that briefly caught his eye but he didn't read the article. The real spun slowly until he stopped on the obituary section; Evron James Brown stared back at him from the page. In the adjacent column was the somber face of Kwong Jon Kim, the man from the coffee shop, the man from his dream – what he had thought was a dream.

***

Mercy's automatic doors hissed open and Dirk stepped onto the hospital's tiled floor slippery with the muddy residual of melted snow. Unsteady on his prosthesis he slipped awkwardly into the arms of a police officer who had followed him in.

"All right there pal?" the officer asked. Dirk straightened himself indignantly and without a word of thanks or go to hell he clomped off.

Seated uncomfortably in a row of cozy adjoining lounge chairs, he waited for his appointment. MacGyver was on the waiting room television, the volume inaudibly low. The outdated National Geographic pile didn't interest him either. He retrieved his billfold and took out the folded obituary he had printed an hour earlier. *Evron James Brown* -- it didn't list a cause of death, just "died suddenly". Mr. Kim's cause of death was listed as heart attack.

A hospital employee dressed in green scrubs backed through an adjacent door. She held the door open with her hip while fluid filled test tubes rattled in the rack held firmly in both hands. When she turned around Dirk knew this was another one. Jaw agape, he stared disbelievingly.

His gaze was fixed until she turned the corner out of sight. Without hesitation, he followed. She waited for the elevator, when it opened they both got on. The employee was a black woman with uncommonly large freckles on her cheek bones. Her eyes were set more widely on her face than was ordinary. He noticed her long skinny fingers had extremely long yellow nails. Dirk followed her off of the elevator trying unsuccessfully to be obscure. His heavy lifeless limb clomped noisily in the echoing hall. The woman disappeared behind a door labeled "lab".

Carla Johnson, in the spring, had been nailed to a cross and burned in the basement of her home. Police initially thought it was a hate crime but later discovered the remnants of a meth lab on the property. The strung-out boyfriend admitted to the crime. Carla's mug was all over the media, local and national. Her unusual features and the repulsive manor of her death made her memorable above other victims of crime. Dirk had no doubt; it was her.

Abruptly, Carla, who now wore a brown wool coat, pushed open the door and walked directly into Dirk tumbling him awkwardly to the floor. Avoiding eye contact she said "excuse me" and kept walking. He was getting up when she looked back over her shoulder. She anxiously pressed the illuminated down arrow on the elevator. As the doors were closing, an arm reached in and they bounced open again. Dirk hobbled aboard. He did not press a button. "You know you knocked me over back there."

"Sorry," said Carla "I didn't mean to."

The elevator door opened and Carla hastened her way to the stairs of the west parking garage. Dirk knew he would lose her; with his bum leg he couldn't keep up. The glass wall near the elevator afforded him a view to lower floors. Two floors down a door was closing. Dirk took the elevator to the second floor. When he stepped into the parking garage he could hear heavy rain slapping the pavement. Perhaps he would wait for her car to pull out then get the plate number or step in front of it or just do whatever he needed to do to get his questions answered.

When no car came he made his way to the stairwell on the far side of the garage. It led directly to the street. The sound of the pounding rain reverberated through parking garage stifling all other sounds including Dirk's clumsy advance. Carla stood at the top of the stairs under the covered balcony, out of the rain. She was watching the street for the bus that would come to the stop below.

Dirk grabbed her arm and she spun around wildly fighting to free herself. He pulled her in close, her back hard against his chest. With his hand over her mouth to keep her from screaming, he growled the words through clenched teeth, "I know who you are Carla." His words were angry, quiet and venomous. "I know *what* you are too. I haven't entirely figured it out, but you're going to help me with that. The way I figure it, when people die they hang around to torment others. Who do you hate Carla, your boyfriend? But he's locked up in jail so what are you doing here? Are you gonna kill someone at the hospital or maybe just torture them? How many like you are there? Is Imo Jean Parker here too, my *beloved* grandmother? Is that old bat still here haunting me?"

Her wide set eyes were filled with terror. She sunk her teeth into the leathered flesh of his palm. When he jerked it away in pain, she broke free and ran for the steps. Dirk lunged after her, caught her by the coat and plunged to his knees. Carla was suspended face first over the steps, dangling in space, secured tenuously by the garment her attacker held. A torrent of rain cascaded off of the back of her head. She watched it splash down the stairs below her. When Dirk tried to stand, his prosthetic leg slid out from under him, her coat slipped from his grip. As he scrambled upright, he heard her tumbling down the steps. At the bottom of the stairs Carla lay in a mixed heap of broken bones and blood. With curiosity and caution he started down the stairs. A sickening feeling of dread instantly perked in his bowels at what horrors might befall him for tormenting what he thought could only be pure evil.

The pool of blood grew quickly as if it flowed from a garden hose. Then, as if someone had let the air out of an inflatable woman, the body began to change. Her clothes sunk slowly down until they clung to bone. Rain drops pecked away the exposed flesh on her arms, hands and face and as the loosened tissue sloughed away the stench of death grew pungent and nauseating. Dirk began to wretch and walked, as quickly as he could, away from the body, into the shadow of the building across the street. The building sheltered him from the rain and supported his quivering frame. He didn't want to be connected to the mess so he moved on in the shadows.

"Fuck, I need a drink!"

The MTA came to a stop at the sign where the body lay. The bus driver opened the door and said "Miss?" He left his seat and went out into the rain.

PART TWO

1

He set down his drink and stared through the haze of cigarette smoke, past the naked, gyrating women, into the solitary realm of memory.

"Jimmy, remember when we were kids and you and Randy thought it'd be cool to beat the hornets nests out of the pig's sty?" Kimmy stood next to her brother who was on his way to a hard drunk. "Man, I don't know why I let my big brother talk me into doing something so stupid." As men shuffled down the aisle in front of the neon runway, between rows of elevated bar stools and wobbly tables, they walked right through her. Seeming not to notice or perhaps to care, she continued, "Like a sixty pound eight year old was gonna actually hold off a three hundred pound charging sow with a straw broom." One man completely occupied her space so she was no longer visible. Then she leaned out of him, her face seaming to morph out of the man's, and looked at her brother. "Shit I don't know what scared me more that maniacal screaming pig or the fifty pissed off wasps." The man walked on. "You and Randy came screaming around the corner of that sty and blew right past me. Man, you just left me behind like a freakin pig speed bump or something. Oh my God, but it was priceless to see two big bullies reduced to screaming little sissy girls." She laughed and shook her head with a reminiscent smile.

Her smile faded as she looked around the dimly lit room. There were two types of patrons, the lecherous old farts who sat alone in dark corners and the raucous young crowd dangling dollar bills at the less than attractive, naked women on stage. "Jim, really – you've made better choices than this place," she scolded.

Jimmy took a big drink and stared, not at the dancers nor at the patrons, just stared... "Shit Kimmy," he said, "you got dealt a rotten hand in life kid." He stood and walked right through her.

Unfazed, Kimmy followed. A malnourished, large breasted woman was entertaining the crowd on the other side of the runway. On the lip of the unattended portion of the stage sat several drinks, some empty – some not. Two guys stood with their back to Jim. They had wandered not far off from the bar stools for a better view. Next to assorted drinks sat a wallet. Jimmy stopped, so did Kimmy.

As Jimmy fixated on the wallet, a light misty fog grew out of the nappy red shag carpet. Kimmy expected a reaction from her brother to this unusual phenomenon but neither he nor anyone else noticed. The fog swirled at his feet then slowly coiled around him. Before it reached his waist it took on a red hue. Oddly, the fog gave off a warm dry breeze. Kimmy protectively held her ground close to Jimmy. A scarlet iridescent human form materialized into a sleek naked woman that danced seductively in front of him. She moved to the music that filled the bar; her hips undulating and her hands feeling up her temptress torso. She leaned in close to Jimmy's ear and whispered, "Take it, you know you want it."

Jimmy's hand went slowly out toward the billfold, passing through the phantom harlot. Kimmy stepped close and shouted "Jimmy No!" A puff of air on the back of his head ruffled his hair. He retracted his hand and reached up to smooth it. The demon woman glared at Kimmy then morphed quickly into a giant eel and struck out at her. Kimmy swiftly somersaulted through the air to avoid contact. The lustrous serpent darted into the crowd and vanished.

On stage a dancer had turned her attention to Jimmy and the men had returned to their bar stools. Jimmy reached into his blue jeans and pulled out a ten dollar bill. He waved it at the dancer. She squatted down in front of him – the G-string bikini bottoms hid no more than was required by law; her tasseled breasts, at eye level. She expected Jimmy to put the ten in her string but he pulled it back and grabbed a handful of titty. The dancer reached between her legs, grabbed a full glass and threw the contents in his face.

Wiping the rain from his face Dirk stepped through the front door of the The Cave and pulled up a chair at the first empty table just as two large men escorted Jimmy forcefully from the building.

PART TWO

2

With a damp towel, Alex mopped the heavily chlorinated water from his face. He liked to swim at the Y late at night. It was an easy walk from his grandmother's apartment so, on the rare occasions he got away from Ames, he would slip out to swim after his grandmother had gone to bed. After 10PM family swimmers had retired and if there was anyone there they were generally serious swimmers and kept quietly to themselves.

***

Amelia stepped off of the bus and walked three blocks to the YMCA. It was the first time she had ventured "in body" outside of the Harger Blish. Kimmy on her own adventure to the art store, would be waiting for her at Pop's coffee shop at midnight. She went to the counter and simply said, "Pool," as she slid the clerk the required denomination.

Setting down her tan canvas garment bag in front of a locker, she unzipped it and pulled out a beige suit and swim cap. The familiar smell of chlorine penetrated the quiet room coaxing fond memories from her darkened cerebral closet. Astray in random recollections, she turned to walk to the dressing stall and gasped out loud as she almost ran over another woman.

"Oh my," the surprised woman gasped. "Excuse me, I don't often run into other women here this late. This place needs a little more estrogen," the woman said with a surprised and pleasant tone. "Are you going to be coming here regularly?" With a cute, boyish and naturally pretty appeal, the young woman's curly blonde hair and big smiling brown eyes invited conversation the way a puppy invited petting.

Amelia struggled with the rules of in body encounters which discouraged both conversation and eye contact. "I don't know when I'll be back. I'm just here visiting for a short time. Excuse me," she said as she brushed hurriedly past. The woman was bewildered by the lack of conversation. She shrugged, dropped her bag on the floor next to a locker and walked out to the pool through the access door.

When Amelia had dressed she took her clothes back to her bag and stuffed them inside. She saw the woman's blue denim gym bag next to a locker. DSM PD was printed on the side in yellow block letters.

There were eight lap lanes six were roped off for use. Lanes 1-4 were in use. She heard the diving board wobble and saw Alex Garreth complete a half pike before he pierced the water.

It had been four years, almost to the day, when she had first met Alex at this same location. He had introduced himself as Billy. It was a defining event in her young life, never before had she allowed the level of intimacy she shared that night. The fact that there had been no follow-up phone call broke her heart. The fact that he was introduced at her first ISU swim team practice as Alex, *not* Billy, made her fume.

She plunged into the open lap lane, intent on wiping her mind of memories; she focused on form as she broke into a rigorous freestyle. Her body lithely rotated with every arm stroke so that the shoulder of her recovering arm was higher than the shoulder of her pulling arm. As one shoulder fell, it aided the arm catching the water, as one shoulder raised it aided the arm at end of the push to leave the water. At the wall she executed a flawless somersault, throwing her legs toward the wall and gliding off of one toward the next.

Finishing five hundred meters, Amelia popped out of the water. Breathing hard from a vigorous workout, she grabbed the pools edge and took a break. It had been several months since she had been in a pool; the day of her life altering and eventually life ending accident.

She felt strong, invigorated and ironically full of life. After a few minutes at pool side she turned to begin her second set. Across the pool they made eye contact. Alex starred with a quizzical gaze.

"Contact with anyone from your past is strictly forbidden and will be met with immediate and severe consequences." The words quoted from *the book,* by the little man in the brown suite and bolo, were consciously audible. She dove under the water and tried again to wipe Alex from her thoughts. He watched as the unidentifiable, yet familiar woman executed a powerful and perfect freestyle stroke. He watched the swimmer and the clock and wondered for which collegiate team she swam.

Forty minutes later she sat on the pool's edge and dabbed at the stray droplets of water, lost in thought, wondering which had been more exhausting, exercising her body or exercising emotional restraint. Exasperated she muttered, "Good God, of all of the people to be here, why Alex?" She watched him discretely from behind her towel as she dried her face. Every muscle movement was accentuated on his glistening skin as he walked toward the diving board. He had the hardest gastrocnemius she had ever seen, flat, taught and defined; like two bricks had replaced his calves. His gluteus maximus was also a sight to behold.

She closed her eyes, buried her face in the towel and rubbed vigorously at her forehead as if trying to scrub away the memory of Alex. It worked; another more recent memory came to mind.

"No interaction allowed with anyone from your past. You will lose your body form privileges." Evron Brown warned Kimmy and Amelia as they left the building. On the steps of the Harger Blish, bundled in similar brown winter coats, she hugged her friend before they walked in opposite directions toward separate bus stops. Amelia dropped her coins into the bus meter. The driver looked up to see a round-faced young woman of average height and build bundled in plain brown clothes. Neither Kimmy nor Amelia, or any former living person out in public, would resemble their former self. By description they would be plain, average and unremarkable to a living person.

The dive board bounced once, then again but the sound that followed was unexpected… a thud and wobble of the board before an awkward splash. She waited. Alex didn't come up. Two men in the closest lanes swam frantically toward the diver. Amelia dropped her towel and ran to the board. The water was red with blood… lots of blood. One man climbed out of the pool while the other hoisted Alex's limp and bleeding body from the pool. They laid him on the floor but neither man knew what to do next.

Pushing the men aside, Amelia dropped to her knees. "Call an ambulance." She ordered. The other woman in the pool had just pulled herself out and still dripping sprinted from the room. Amelia checked for a pulse as the blood spilled from his head wound and puddled around her knees. No pulse. She straddled him while the two men watched helplessly. "Come on Alex stay with me." She choked back the tears and started chest compressions. "One - one thousand, two - one thousand, three - one thousand….. breathe." She pinched his nose and blew into his mouth. The chest did not rise. She repeated One – one thousand, two…. with each breath the chest again refused to rise.

Suddenly brown leather boots appeared to be standing on the blood…not in the blood. She looked up, her face flush and streaked with tears. Evron said "Amelia, you're dead. A dead person can't breathe life into someone else." She looked at the faces of the men around her – they didn't see Evron. The woman returned and calmly said, "Help is coming. I'm a police officer." She looked at Amelia and said, "Are you trained in CPR?" Amelia scrambled off Alex. "Go get a towel," she calmly directed, "and apply pressure to the wound."

Amelia started for the locker room but Evron stepped in front of her. "You can't interfere and you can't be questioned. You need to leave." She looked back at the swimmers gathered around Alex's limp bloody form then sprinted past Evron to the locker room. When she ran back with the towel she pressed it forcefully into the hands of the closest person. She hesitated only for a moment, hoping to see his lungs fill before she retreated to the locker room. She dressed quickly and heard the ambulance approaching as she left the building. On the street she rounded the corner of the Y and stood in the dark, sobbing.

***

Alex stepped into the light and moved gradually forward through the tranquil fog. He found himself standing before a large window. A white marble countertop separated Alex from an ordinary looking black woman. The woman wore no jewelry, she wore no makeup, and she wore no expression. She wore white clothing.

"Alex Garreth, age twenty-one. Cause of death, head trauma." She smiled, "You have been accepted into the gates of heaven. You may remain close to earth if you wish to comfort those who grieve for you or you may enter heaven directly. Kindly follow the white line to the waiting ferry for your passage or you may take the blue line to the comfort house to await further instructions."

Alex turned instinctively to the white line. He walked onto the luscious, green riverbank and into the warm sun. A ferry waited at a dock just up the bank of the beautiful river. To his left was a bridge. It was divided into two lanes by a blue line. At the crest of the bridge was Amelia; beautiful and healthy.

She had returned to the Harger Blish, to the train and to the registration center expecting to see Alex; her hopes were conflicting. She wanted to see him again, to touch him and to explain what she had felt for the past several years. She also hoped that she would not see him, both for fear of the confrontation and for the fate that would be his. She was searching for the right thing to say if she met him... then suddenly, there he was. Nothing, absolutely nothing came to mind. She panicked. She ran.

PART TWO

3

Kimmy stepped off of the bus with a brown paper sack clutched to her chest. It contained charcoal pencils and sketch pads. She walked two blocks to the dimly lit café. The hand painted sign on the shop window exclaimed in mustard yellow pastel "Pop's Diner" "HOT COFFEE 24 - 7". A half dozen people sat collectively alone. The clock on the wall said 11:50. Amelia was nowhere in sight so she sat at an open table that faced the door. An older couple sat quietly staring in different directions, involved in their separate thoughts. A diminutive young tow headed man, reading a faded and dog eared copy of 20,000 Leagues Under the Sea was accompanied by an Asian man, maybe fiftyish; his fuzzy dark hair was combed in an attempt to mask a wide scar across his forehead. He busied himself by discreetly trimming his nails below the table.

She wondered how many of these people were "in body". Pop's had been on the list of late night services which came with their clothing and allowance. The coffee was warm and welcoming on a chilly winter night. Funny, in life she never liked the stuff, but she had drained the cup without noticing as she sketched the occupants of the diner. The clock said 12:20 when she got up to refill her cup. Over her shoulder she heard the door open. Expecting to see Amelia she looked instead at the familiar face of a man she couldn't yet place. He wore a dirty blue work shirt and dingy jeans. Attempting to avoid eye contact, she lowered her gaze and returned to her table. Thump, thud,…. thump thud. She kept her head down; eyes averted and busied herself with her sketch pad. Then she got it - it was the pissed off one legged man that she'd seen in physical therapy.

"Hey Max, sign here," he said as he handed the clerk a delivery bill. While Max studied the bill, Dirk surveyed the café. A look of recognition came across his face. He was staring at Kwong Jon Kim. After Max had returned the signed bill, Dirk set his course passing directly in front of Kimmy. Once he passed, she looked up from her sketchpad. His left leg seemed heavier than the right and made a clicking noise. Dirk stopped at the table where the duo sat. He flipped back the papers on his clip board "This is you ain't it?" he said to the

Asian man as he tapped the exposed page. Both men looked up from their books.

Kimmy couldn't see from her vantage point but Dirk had an obituary with a picture of the patron. "You're Kwong Jon Kim ain't ya?" The man said nothing.

"Buddy, that's an obituary," the young companion responded. "I think you've got the wrong guy."

"I'm not out of my fuckin mind… I've seen him before. And I ain't talking to you, ya little shit, so shut the fuck up."

All of the patrons were interested now. Kimmy tried not to look directly at the confrontation; however, what the limping man had said certainly did interest her. She pretended to sketch but glanced inconspicuously over her paper at the confrontation.

He leaned across the table and asked in a low and menacing voice, "Who are you here for? Who did you come to haunt, you freak?" The younger man stood and gently touched his friend's arm. "Let's go Tom." They started to leave when Dirk thrust the table at them both. Coffee cups shattered and the Asian man fell forward onto the shards. Immediately blood trickled from his hand.

Max hurried between Dirk and the wrecked table. He yelled "Get out of here Dirk and don't ever come back. I'm calling your boss about this." A young man in a dingy damp apron emerged from the back room and he and Max herded Dirk through the front door. Before the accident, Dirk would have clobbered the two but his new appendage still had him off balance, his brawling days were done.

Outside the café, he refused to leave. He'd wait for another chance. The younger man grabbed his jacket and wrapped the sleeve around the other's bleeding hand. The cut didn't look that bad but there was an awful lot of blood. "He's a hemophiliac, we gotta get to the hospital can you get us a cab?

"Do you want an ambulance?" asked Max.

"No just call a cab."

Max picked up the clip board that lay on the floor – the obituary exposed. "Man, he's a fruit loop, this doesn't look anything like you."

Kimmy quickly downed her coffee as an excuse to go for a refill. She walked by the table where the young man was trying to stop the bleeding and discretely examined the picture. It was him. She filled her cup and returned to the table. Noticing the clock said 12:30, she decided to go in search of Amelia, and in doing so, remove herself from what could potentially become a scene of public disturbance. She gathered her drawings and went to the door. The cab was just arriving. "Cab's here," she announced.

Dirk was out of the line of sight, hiding just behind the opening door. When Kimmy opened the door for the two exiting patrons, she accidentally hit Dirk with it, knocking him backward and into the building. The open door and Kimmy's presence blocked his advance.

Dirk lunged forward and tried to maneuver around her. She tried to move forward causing him to lurch more to try to get around her. It was an awkward dance. He growled, "Get the fuck away from me."

His face turned from anger to stunned recognition... the girl from therapy, the girl from the papers, the girl... Kimmy Shobek, who had gruesomely murdered her quadriplegic hospital roommate before killing herself too. "You!" he said, "It's you!"
She sprinted past.

Redirecting his attention, Dirk reached the cab as the door closed. The cabbie had locked it. The young man flipped him off as the cab drove away. The long, thick, square nail of the offending finger brought a look of understanding to Dirk's face. He recalled the hospital bed and the long thick fingernails of Evron, the orderly. He knowingly nodded. Max and the dishwasher stood glaring.
"Piss off," Dirk growled and clomped back to his delivery truck.

PART TWO

4

DSM PD glistened in yellow reflective letters on the brow of Detective Laurie Crandall's navy ball cap. Upon arriving at Mercy she held open the lobby door so that a man could wheel an ailing woman to a waiting car. "Thanks," said the man she would never know as Harlen. Laurie had tucked her blonde, damp, chlorine saturated hair, under her ball cap so that the only exposed portion was the golden soaked ponytail which hung limp through the opening. The feeble woman in the wheel chair studied Laurie then burst into tears.

In her six years as a homicide investigator for the Des Moines Police Department she had seen a lot of death; she hadn't seen many people die. She followed the corridors of the hospital to the emergency room.

"Hey Laurie, what are you doing here?" asked the young nurse at the registration desk.

"Hey Donna. There was a kid that was brought in with a head injury not long ago… a swimming accident. I just wanted to check his status."

"You're not on duty are ya?"

"No. I was at the Y when he got hurt. I gave him CPR but I never got him back. I was hoping the paramedics did."

"That was Robin's case. Let me see if I can find her." The nurse left her station and disappeared around the corner. After a short while a young woman in wrinkled green scrubs appeared.

"Hey Laurie." said Robin. "The kid with the head injury, the swimmer," she leaned against the wall, "he didn't make it."

"Shit." Laurie grimaced with an exasperated sense of failure.

"If he had, he wouldn't have had much of a life. He left a good chunk of his brain in the pool. Sorry, the medics said you were there. Nothing you could have done would have helped," Robin attempted to comfort. "Todd's here," she said cheerfully, intending to lighten the mood. "He just brought in a DUI. The guy tried to escape on foot but fell face first into a tree. They're stitching him up so Todd can take him back to the station. He's in eight," she said referring to the ER room numbers.

Laurie noticed the darkened circles beneath Robins tired eyes. "You look beat."

"Yeah, three hours to go – it's been a long night." The emergency room doors swung open and medics wheeled in another. Robin pushed off of the wall and groaned as she walked toward the approaching gurney.

Laurie waved at the nurse's station as she walked past to the exam room. She looked through the window and saw a patient, whom she would never know as Jimmy Shobek, strapped firmly to the bed. A doctor stitched a large gash on the patient's forehead. Todd Round's leg made a triangle against the exam room wall where he appeared to support it with the muscular bulk of his torso. He had been blessed with a physique that was bulked with little effort to maintain. Sensing her stare, he glanced up from his dutiful watch to see the familiar brown eyes of the woman he loved.

Todd motioned to the assisting nurse that he was going out, the nurse replied with a nod. In the hall, he put his hands on Laurie's hips and bent to kiss her forehead. "What are you doing here?" he said with a little concern in his voice.

"A kid got hurt at the pool tonight. I came to check on him."

"A kid! How old?" Todd asked with genuine concern. He loved children; would have liked to have a dozen but Laurie had a medical issue that they both knew would keep her from fulfilling that desire.

"Well, a kid by my middle age standards, College age I'd say."

"How is he?"

"Yeah...," she said regretfully but trying to sound unaffected. "He didn't make it. I'll tell you about it at home , I just wanted to say hi."

Her cover didn't work with him. They'd been together too long for that veil to be effective. He changed the subject. "So... any leads on the rotting corpse from last night?"

Her face lit up with excitement when she realized she hadn't told him. "Holy shit, you're not gonna believe it! The stiff was Carla Johnson!"

"The burned at the cross Carla Johnson?" he said disbelievingly.

"The same!" Agreeing with his look of confusion, "I know!" she said in an exaggerated voice. "The press is going to have a field day with this one. It's just too creepy. I've been trying to get my mind around this case all night, and you know my mind works better after a good workout - or good sex ...and since you weren't home I figured I better go to the pool."

"Good choice," he smirked.

Her pager buzzed on her belt. "I gotta call in. Give me a squeeze when you crawl in bed tonight." She hurried back to the nurse's station.

After listening to the call and taking hurried notes, she raced out of the hospital. Laurie sped from the parking lot so quickly that she nearly collided with a metro bus.

PART TWO

5

"Son of a bitch," cursed the bus driver having barely missed the dark sedan racing up the dimly lit, damp street. Kimmy crawled around on the vehicle floor collecting her pencils.

"You ok?" he asked. Kimmy was the only passenger on board and this was the last run of the night.

She nodded yes and sat again with her back to the window, her knees up, her sketch pad flat against her thighs. The butterfly birthmark quivered as if it would take flight as she frantically sketched out scenes from the coffee shop: The Asian man falling onto broken shards of the coffee cups remains, the clerk yelling at the hobbling aggressor, the raging face of the same man as he confronted her behind the protective door of the coffee shop. The images rapidly spilled from her pencil and onto the pages like she was trying to pour them from her mind. She glanced out the window at the soiled snow covered sidewalks and passing darkened buildings then packed away her drawings. She pushed the vertical rubber strip that rang the bell alerting the bus driver to stop.

When Kimmy stepped off of the rear exit of the bus, she quickly walked into the shadows of the surrounding structures. It was a three block walk to the Harger Blish. When Kimmy approached the side entrance to the building she glanced around to see if anyone was about. Then she opened the door and went in.

In the lobby she saw Amelia take a young man's hand and enter the auditorium. Puzzled by her friend's affection for this person but anxious to unburden herself of the evening's events she hurried back to her room.

Alex had stepped from the train and entered the Harger Blish in search of Amelia. Now they stood face to face and neither could find the words.

"I lost it," he said finally to break the silence.

Amelia said nothing; she didn't understand what he was trying to say. "What had he lost?" she wondered.

Sad and apologetic he said, "Your number, Millie... I lost it."

It had been four years since he had called her Millie, or even acknowledged that he knew her. She had harbored the conflicting emotions of resentment and infatuation ever since. And now, post mortem, they had the mutual courage to admit their faults.

"Only my family calls me Millie," she said. Where'd the name Billy come from?"

"It was my grandfather's name; my middle name is William. My Grandma is the only person who calls me..... Oh no! Grandma! I gotta find her." The auditorium doors opened.

"You will, I'll help you," she said reassuringly.

As the new arrivals filtered past them, Amelia took Alex's hand and walked with him into the auditorium.

Feeling refreshed by the steamy shower, Kimmy went about the task of hygienic maintenance. She trimmed her hair and clipped her nails into the waste basket. Her file was not where she thought she had left it but she recalled that she had slipped it into her backpack when she had left earlier. When she opened the bag her recent sketch stared back at her; a warm nauseating sensation overcame her. It wasn't just the jolting reminder of her confrontation but also the warning she recalled upon her orientation.
"Nothing comes into the Harger Blish which was not issued to you from within. Any outside contraband is strictly forbidden and will be met with immediate and severe consequences."

Amelia entered the room conflicted and confused by the events of the evening. She was even more perplexed to see that Kimmy had a similar look. They briefly exchanged silent, mutual, yet personal, bewilderment before a startling knock at the door jolted them into their skins.

Evron James Brown looked pointedly at each of the girls. Each was certain Evron had come for her violation which was promised to be "immediate and severe."

"Come with me," he instructed and both followed.

"What are you doing?" Amelia asked her friend with some regret in her voice. "He wants me."

"No, I'm pretty sure it's me," said Kimmy with a resolute sigh.

"Both of you," he emphasized, "come with me."

Alex arrived just as the solemn parade passed. Fearful for Amelia's fate he quickly stepped in front of Evron and proclaimed, "Whatever it is you think she did, she didn't. She didn't violate any of the rules." Evron did not respond but stared blankly into Alex's determined eyes. "Wherever you're taking her, I'm going too," he firmly insisted.

Evron shrugged in a 'suit yourself manner' and proceeded down the hall. Kimmy raised a brow to Amelia and smirked. Now the parade was four. The group proceeded to a large and lavish library. It was stacked to the high ceiling with four walls of books. The royal blue wool carpet was unusually thick. It absorbed the noise so much that even the closing of the heavy door was barely audible. Beautifully detailed tiffany floor lamps illuminated overstuffed scarlet wingback chairs which were tucked into the private corners of the room. In one chair sat a small man.

Evron motioned the group to be seated at an ornate table in the center of the room; inlayed wood of many varieties formed an intricate star of David on the table's top. In a firm and sullen voice he explained the situation.

"Boys and Girls we have a seer in our midst; an unpleasant one. A seer is a living person who can see the dead. Some see only the out of body souls, others can identify the physical forms of the living person rather than the common unidentifiable form projected to others. Some seers are ordained; their gift has a purpose and they generally accept and use their gift as they know instinctively they should. Others develop the ability to become a seer through catastrophic events such as a near death experience. In this case the seer believes the perished individuals he identifies are still on earth to terrorize and he has become a vigilante determined to take out all he identifies. He has identified three in this room; myself, Kimmy and Charlie." He motioned to the man who sat quietly in the corner. Kimmy recognized the petite young man from the coffee shop. He had accompanied his badly bleeding friend into the cab.

"Dirk Cooper is responsible for the extermination of two souls. The soul of Carla Johnson, who was serving a purgatory sentence as a hospital aide, was extinguished when she was brutally attacked in the parking garage of Mercy hospital last night. The rotting carcass of the soul which was Kwong Jon Kim lies outside of the Harger Blish tonight. As was discussed in orientation, it is vital to protect your vessel from harm. The fluid that fills it keeps it supple. Without liquid the deceased vessel quickly decays and without protection of a sanctioned dwelling, the soul is lost…. forever. Dirk Cooper is also responsible, although not entirely, for the loss of my life."

"That was you!" Kimmy exclaimed. "The fight at the packing plant; I was there in the crowd that nigh!" she continued with a more subdued amazement. "I'd never been to a fight before but my friend Trash was a big fan of yours. After that night I swore I'd never go to another --- it was brutal. Holy shit… I didn't know you died."

Evron stared at Kimmy wondering if she had been that last person ever to see him alive. The others pondered the situation. Up to that moment each had known that their own actions had consequence in death but never had they thought someone else's actions might impact their life ever after – or lack thereof.

Evron continued, "This place is right now crawling with cops. The driver reported the large quantity of blood in his taxi to his dispatch. The location of the drop was given to the police. They've already discovered Mr. Kim's decomposed body at the building's entrance."

"It's not likely that any of the police are seers but we are going to take every precaution to limit contact. We're doubling up on rooms and confining everyone to their quarters until further notice. Alex, you'll be bunking with Charlie. Aren't you glad you invited yourself?"

PART TWO

6

"I'm sorry Lieutenant, there's no way to track the blood trail in this kind of weather. This is the damnedest rain I've ever seen in February; it's coming down in buckets," the officer recounted on the radio from the dry sanctuary of the squad car. The Lieutenant's response was drowned out by an excited rapping at the car window. The Sergeant rolled down his window and another rain soaked officer adorned in a standard issue yellow slicker spoke loudly to be heard over the slapping of the rain against the pavement.

"We got a body, but it ain't the guy we're lookin for. This one's been dead a while – a long while. He's out behind the Harger Blish."

Swirling lights flashed yellow and red against the exterior of the abandoned building. Detective Crandall and two forensics team members hovered over the corpse. The rain had stopped but the temperature was falling fast. "This body is going to be frozen to the stoop if we don't get it out of here," Laurie said. "I want pictures from every angle and get a close up of the clothing head to toe. Something's strange. The tissue decay would indicate he's at least six to eight weeks dead but his clothes aren't even soiled."

"Maybe the rain washed him clean," said the teammate collecting and logging the debris at the scene: old cigarette butts, cellophane wrappers, discarded garbage typical of litter in the area.

"Get a picture of his shoes. They're barely scuffed. A pair of loafers like that wouldn't last long if any of the mission guys had found him. I don't understand why they didn't; this place is generally hopping with hobos."

"You're thinking Carla Johnson, aren't ya?" said Tom Hawthorn, the detective with whom she shared an office. He had shown up on the scene partly as a courtesy, mostly out of curiosity. Laurie was Senior Detective and it was entirely her show.

She slid Tom a look that said she agreed then flipped up her collar and blew warmth into her hands. "Let's get him bagged and over to the coroner while we can still get him off the pavement." The pavement was becoming slick with ice. "Sergeant, see if your men can track down any of the homeless that shelter in this building. I'm

145

heading over to the coroner's office to fill in the details. Let me know who you find in there."

It was 2:20 AM when the Polk County Coroner entered the morgue at Des Moines General. He carried a steaming Styrofoam cup of Quick Trip java and looked like he had been on the uphill side of forty winks not long ago. He blew across the cup and took a sip then shook his head like a wet dog shaking off the rain.

He photographed the body bag before slipping on his plastic over coat, rubber gloves and paper mask. Laurie laid out the details of discovery without her speculations of the case similarity. He unzipped the bag and a putrid stench filled the air. The tissue which had covered the cheek bones and forehead had become disconnected in transport and exposed the whiteness of the bones.

He touched the corpse's undamaged garment and shot Laurie a look. "Wow. This looks grotesquely familiar," he said before flipping on the tape recorder which lay near him on a table of trade tools.

Laurie covered her mouth and wretched as she took one step back from the odor. "No need to stay, I know how to reach you. I'll call with the findings." With that she left him alone to find the clues which would identify this latest decomposed mystery.

It was after 10AM when the phone rang in her apartment. "He's Asian, based on the brachycephalic head shape, absent brow ridge, small nasal apertures and projecting zygomas, I'd say Korean. There's a three inch horizontal laceration at the center of the frontal bone. You want the weirdest part? He was embalmed, wait… it gets stranger, the fluid is red. Embalming fluid is yellow, why would anyone dye it? Additionally, there's no evidence of infestation so I'd say this guy's been in an airtight box. Given that information, when I estimated the rate of decomposition I'd say he's been dead twelve to fourteen weeks. He's had some work done on his teeth. I sent the x-rays out about an hour ago. The clothing is another oddity, there's almost no embedded dirt. Looks like the guy got up and dressed himself this morning. My job is to provide you with facts… and the fact is this is very similar to Carla Johnson."

"Certainly sounds like it, doesn't it? Anything else?"

"I found a three centimeter shard of porcelain imbedded between the lunate and scaphoid of the left hand."

"In English please."

"The wrist," he stated. "There are letters on the shard… Po; that's a capital p and a lowercase o like a proper noun. I sent it over to forensics along with the clothing. I'll get you more details when they're available. "

As she was hanging up the phone, Todd shuffled from the bedroom shielding his eyes from the glaring sunlight. He had a bad case of bed head and yawned widely as he stretched and groaned out a good morning. When he had come home at 4AM he discovered Laurie asleep on the couch, pictures of the two investigations scattered on the coffee table. Todd had draped an afghan over her before he put himself to bed.

Glancing from the strewn papers and pictures and back to Laurie his eyes asked the question for him. To which she responded, "We've got another rotten corpse and the similarities are too glaring to dismiss."

PART TWO

7

Out of body visits relieved the monotony of lockdown. Amelia was with her mother and father every hour she was allowed. Esther still cried, but less frequently. She and Harlen openly displayed affection more than Amelia previously recalled. Through subtle warm touches and frequent hand holding, they gave each other strength.

Kimmy spent time with her brother, her Dad and her good friend Margie. She learned that Jimmy had attached himself to a frail young coma patient at Mercy. At first this troubled Kimmy; it seemed he was setting himself up for another hard fall but this little girl was an ear that would not judge him. He quietly poured forth emotions no one else would be privileged to hear. Her silence was cathartic, allowing him to express and relieve his troubled mind. Unbeknownst to him an attending nurse regularly and furtively listened to his private conversations using the time to let loose her own pent up emotions. He often flirted with the nurse and a healthy relationship seemed to be growing. Jimmy was more frequently sober.

Kimmy also gained some enlightening insight into her father's extremely private and pathological world. When he drove his truck he talked to himself; not always to himself, also to Kimmy and to her mother. How long had he been talking to her mother she wondered... and could she hear him from her KP duties at the Harger Blish?

"Looking lovely today Mary. Is that a new dress? I see you and Kimmy are having a good time. I assume you have discount stores there in heaven; you two must have been shopping. No, I don't mind; spend all the money you want. Could you maybe send me some of that cash? The old El Camino could use some new tires. Kimmy, you been drawing any of those pictures for your Momma? She's a terrific artist ya know, Mary. I got every picture she ever drew me, and some she didn't draw for me but I rescued from the trash anyhow. Now... don't give me any of that Kimmy – you're better than any artist I've ever seen. You got real talent." He conversed that way from Ankeny to Peoria; three hours without a lull.

In the total of Kimmy's entire life she had not heard him speak so many words. Social isolation, lack of conversation and limited emotional expression... Kimmy had no idea her father was schizophrenic. Functionally schizoid, it appeared. She wondered if it was the drugs he and Mary had done or maybe Vietnam. She liked having these conversations with him.

"Dad, I had no idea you liked my drawings. Do you still have the…"

"Circus Peanuts! That's my favorite Kimmy. The one you drew with the two little boys at the Big Top circus in Park Fair. The little guys were sharing a bag of peanuts; you captured the look of sheer panic when that elephant reached his big old trunk between them."

She happily picked up her part of the conversation and continued their chat; thankful to finally understand him and to realize that she had always possessed his love and approval. She listened, responded, smiled and cried.

***

The knock at the door startled Amelia. Police wouldn't have knocked on a door in an abandoned building. She was pretty sure there wasn't really even a door that would be visible to the living eye. Earlier in the lockdown a uniformed officer had entered the room. He didn't open a door; rather he passed right through it. He also passed through Kimmy as she lay in a trance on the bed. When his flashlight sought out Amelia she darted to the safety of a dark corner to avoid the beam's penetration. At that instant she noticed a piece of paper flitter through Kimmy's backpack landing on the officer's shoe.

Startled by the movement he had rapidly searched the corners with his beam for whatever had caused the paper to flutter that way. Finding no one, he retrieved the paper and observed the remarkably well sketched face of an enraged man. The pencil strokes caught the tight lines around his clenched jaw; even the stains on his jagged teeth were visible. "Remarkable detail," he privately commented. He shined his light at Kimmy's pack then reached through the pack, which he had not observed, and produced a brown paper sack with pencils and various other drawings. Stuffing the bag under his arm he again passed through the door and out of sight.

"Tap, tap, tap." Again the knock was soft, as if to be inconspicuous. Alex stood alone in the darkened, deserted hallway. When the door opened he quickly stepped in not waiting for an invitation, not wanting to be caught out of his quarters.

"This place is spooky when it's silent, even for a ghost," he quipped. Happy to see him but concerned that he would take such a risk, she reprimanded him for breaking the rules. Alex picked up the copy of "The Book" that lay on the dresser. He turned it over in his hands to observe the wear. Obviously the book had been well used. The pages were dog eared and the binding was creased. He looked at Kimmy laced and stiff in her bed.

Running his fingers through his curly crown he landed in an exasperated sprawl on Amelia's bed. "I can't do it," he said in defeat. "I've been watching Charlie jump around in his trance visiting all of his relatives for three days and I can't do it. I've read the book – I know what I'm supposed to do but I can't make it work. Every time I close my eyes all I see is you."

Amelia didn't hide her warm smile. It was their individual tendencies to hide emotion in life that kept them apart. Now, in this brief moment in time, the best they could do was to hide nothing. She lay down next to him on the bed and stared at the ceiling. Holding his hand she said "where shall we go?"

"My Grandma lives about a mile from here; a subsidized high rise apartment building on SW 5th and Tuttle. We've been there since my Grandpa died in 76. Grandpa was a truck driver, ran off the road in an ice storm. My mom died when I was born. I guess she never said who my dad was and grandma never pushed her. My mother was Thelma and William's only child. The social security from their deaths was all the money we had to live on."

"We live in a drafty, fourth floor, two room apartment. The plumbing is bad, and even though the furnace runs all winter, it's never warmer than sixty-six degrees. The air conditioner is a window unit that hasn't worked in five years. During the day, the big rigs blast their horns and the fork lifts backfire, but it's quiet at night. The area is mostly industrial so there's not a lot of traffic in and out after business hours." Alex closed his eyes and continued to reminisce.

"Aside from the maintenance issues it's an alright place to grow up. On clear summer nights when The Oaks were playing at Sec Taylor Stadium, me and grandma used to go up to the roof top and listen to the games. You couldn't see the field but you could see the lights. I remember the night in '76 when The Oaks, who weren't greatest that year but not the worst team in the league, beat the Omaha Royals, the best team in the league. Grandma hated the Royals. Her sister Helen lived in Omaha and was always bragging about how much better they were. Anyway, I never saw grandma so spry. She was up out of that lawn chair sailing across the roof top like she was running the bases herself." He smiled to himself as he lay on the bed fingers absently caressing Amelia's as he chatted. Amelia was enjoying his touch and his quiet self-exposure which reminded her of a night that was neither long ago nor far away from the moment they now shared.

"Back then she hadn't let her beautician talk her into that blue hair yet. She still had some pepper in her curly silver hair." A vision of his grandmother running the roof top bases was plainly in his mind and he nearly chuckled as he explained, with great detail, her antics. He described how a frail woman of ninety pounds snatched up his eight year old body and hugged him so tightly that he thought his ribs would surely bust, rocking him back and forth so that his feet swung to and fro off the ground.

Now she hugged Alex's high school graduation picture and rocked back and forth in a sturdy Amish rocker; her tightly coiffed hair was a pale shimmering blue beneath a solitary floor lamp. Amelia clutched Alex's hand in the dimly lit living room that smelled of mothballs and hairspray.

The old woman's rocker halted. As if gently laying a sleeping child to bed, she cradled the framed photo into her lap and studied it through sad, watery eyes that remembered but did not cry. Her breath came and went in rapid threads as she attempted to steady herself against a cascade of emotions.

"Grandma," he said softly, releasing Amelia to kneel by the woman's rocker, "this is Amelia. I would have liked for you to have met under different circumstances. I know you worried about me because I never let other people get close," his words were tender and he looked upon this woman with love and respect, "but I did once. A few years ago I met this intelligent, passionate, beautiful girl. We talked and laughed the entire night like we had known each other a lifetime. There was an energy between us like I had never experienced before. Because I carelessly misplaced a small scrap of paper, I lost her, and because of a tragic accident I thought I had lost her forever. She's here with me grandma. So you don't have to worry; I'm not alone."

Amelia fought back her own tears when Alex confessed his feelings to his grandmother. She approached the pair and affectionately ran her fingers through his curls before she knelt next to him and made her own confession.

"Your grandson and I have a lot in common. Making friends was a struggle for me. I didn't really develop typical child behaviors, maybe because I grew up an only child; isolated on a farm. I was only exposed to children my age in a classroom, except for my cousin who I usually saw only at holidays. She was the closest thing I had to a friend. We had nothing in common and certainly wouldn't have chosen each other." She rambled uncomfortably towards her point. "The point I'm trying to make is that I chose your grandson. The minute we met I felt an attraction. Conversation came easily, unlike it had before with anyone my age. He made me aware of the woman I had grown into. It was an amazing evening we spent together." She redirected her attention to Alex and stared into his eyes as she continued.

"I was crushed beyond words when no phone call came. When fate put us both on the Iowa State swim team and I found out he had given me an alias that night, I tried to hate him but often found myself day dreaming about what had been. My brain wanted to loath but my heart still loved." She continued speaking to the grandmother but intently searched Alex for a response as she spoke. "I know now that the name he gave me was an intimate invitation. He gave me the name that only you have for him and that was an offering that I did not understand until recently. It's ironic that we've discovered so much about our lives in death."

Grandma's breaths were becoming longer, deeper and more relaxed. "You enjoy yourself on the other side," she said. "Grab hold of your new life and live it. I'll meet you on the other side Billy and I wanna see you smilin' when I get there." She kissed her fingers then pressed them to his picture.

A matted toy poodle, the color of lightly milked tea, had been asleep on a couch pillow near the warmth of the heat register. "Here Gee Gee," Alex called. The dog responded and he waived her up onto his Grandma's lap.

She stroked the dog's head. "Oh Gee Gee, he's happy now."

PART TWO

8

Sunday's Des Moines Register Headlines screamed, "Another Decaying Body Discovered," exposing the Harger Blish as the point of discovery. The area was littered with cops and yellow caution tape. Dirk would have to wait until the police activity let up before he could enter the old building for some investigation of his own. By noon Detective Laurie Crandall's team had put together their preliminary findings and were preparing to compare notes before the Division of Criminal Investigation showed up. The DCI was created to provide investigative support and expertise to law enforcement agencies across the state. They were automatically tagged when the body was discovered. The DCI managed the crime lab, toxicology, trace evidence and evidence recovery. Their function: to aid police in the investigation. The key word being *aid*, not control; contrary to the belief of Drake Meyer, Special Agent in charge of DCI's Zone 1. Drake had completed the DCI's Basic Academy in 1984 and had been assigned to DCI Zone four which covered Cedar Rapids and Iowa City. Despite numerous Cedar Rapids Police Department (CRPD) complaints about his insubordinate behavior, or perhaps because of them, he was transferred to Des Moines in January and was rapidly becoming a thorn in Laurie's backside.

"All right ladies," she announced to a dedicated investigative team comprised entirely of men, "what have we discovered?"

"Neither grave had been disturbed. Glendale Cemetery exhumed both sites for us. The boxes were empty. We had the caskets sent to forensics to sweep for traces of anything that could be a clue. Neither of the boxes looked to have been forced open and there was no observable debris. You'd think at least there'd be some grave dirt. My bet would be the bodies were snatched before the caskets were buried," came the first report from the newest and youngest member of the team.

Tom Hawthorne added, "I spoke with the funeral director. They swear the bodies were in the coffins when they were put in the ground. I got statements from both service directors who sealed them up personally. Then I talked to the hearse driver; oddly it was the same guy who drove for both funerals. He said the immediate family rode with the caskets. The bodies must have been nabbed after – hopefully forensics can come up with something."

To the young eager team member she instructed, "Talk to the cemetery caretaker, get his whereabouts and collaborate it with witnesses. I don't think two bodies from the same cemetery is a coincidence. There's a clue here somewhere. Let's find it."

The team was shutting their binders and preparing to resume their duties when in walked DCI Director Drake Meyer. Well-coiffed, shiny, black hair, pasty skin, white colored shirt; extra starch Laurie guessed. For a man who wanted to be in the field, he dressed as if he wouldn't get dirty. "Have a seat everyone," he announced. "I'd like to get your input on some details." They looked to Laurie and she nodded them all toward the door.

"Keep me posted," she instructed as they left, "I'll bring Mr. Meyer up to speed."

Drake made a dramatic attempt at indignation as he raised his squeaky voice. "I insist you bring them back here so I can complete the details in my report!"

"I have all of their details," she said smiling with a friendly reassuring tone, although she had *wanted* to say, "*Insisting won't do you a damn bit of good you scrawny little bastard – this is MY case.*" Instead she offered an olive branch, "Would you like a cup of coffee?"

Drake's shoulders relaxed slightly as he said, "Black, please."

Laurie whiffed the coffee pot with cautious hesitation. It had a bitter burnt smell that made her nostrils involuntarily slam shut. As she disposed of the dregs and readied to make a new pot she disclosed the details of this morning's meeting with the team. The busy work afforded her the opportunity to focus on something other than Drake's snide demeanor, which made it easier for her to be genial. Carrying two piping fresh mugs to a casual table and chairs near the window overlooking the Des Moines River, she placed one in front of Meyer and settled into the chair opposite from him. "What do you have for me?" she pleasantly inquired.

It disappointed him that he had not been able to ruffle the Chief Investigator's feathers. Offense was his better side of the game. If he had been able to ruffle her into a defensive position then he would be the man in charge, at least for today. Instead he conceded this battle and reciprocated the polite conversation as he disclosed his information from the DCI crime scene investigators.

Producing a one inch, three ring binder complete with color coded tabs and neatly punched, crisp pages, he proudly lay the first volume of his case file in front of her. DCI was all about professionalism, but Meyer was over the top with neatness and presentation. Laurie knew the flawless façade reinforced his belief that DCI was superior to the DSM PD. She shared a commonly held opinion by nearly everyone at the city level, that DCI has too much time on their hands.

He succinctly explained, "You notice the first tab outlines the evidence that was collected at the scene within 50 feet of the body." He continued tab by tab which included titles such as Victim Description, Perimeter 0-50', Perimeter 50.1-100', Witness testimony, Harger Blish History, Interior Findings, Coroner Report, Pending Labs.

The report contained nothing new to the investigation but Laurie now had it in a pretty binder form rather than penciled scratches on a lined yellow note pad. With a patented parting routine, he flattened his tie and crisply offered a hand shake. "Thank you for the coffee. I'll check my schedule to find a convenient time for you to meet with me again. "

Laurie stood and with excessive firmness she shook his hand. "Let's not rush into another appointment until we have something to report." His shoulders tightened again and the color rushed back into the pale imprint Laurie's grip had left on his hand. Without further utterance, he left the room closing the door resolutely behind him.

PART TWO

9

The door creaked very slowly open and Kimmy sheepishly peered into the room. "Hey, Charlie," she whispered, "you in here?" Charlie lay on his twin sized bed in a darkened room. The blinds at the Harger Blish were always drawn. Kimmy could make out the form of the petite man. One arm across his chest, the other draped across his brow as if trying to block intruding light.

"Uh huh," he replied without effort to move.

Not waiting for an invitation, Kimmy slipped further into the room. She observed the small room realizing the layout was much like hers. Bathroom to the right of the entrance, closet on the outside wall of the bath, two twin beds separated by a nightstand with a single small bronze lamp. A dresser along the wall opposite spanned the distance of both beds and was adorned with the matching lamp. At the end of the dresser was a round table and two chairs next to a heavily blinded window. She took a seat in one of the chairs. "Amelia and Alex are sharing a moment; I thought I'd give them some space. I hope you don't mind if I barge in on you."

"Is the lock down over?" he asked without motion.

"No, that's why I didn't knock… didn't want to 'raise the dead', so to speak." Kimmy wasn't deterred by his uninviting behavior; a man of few words would likely also be a man of few emotions, she surmised.

She looked around the generic room for something that would give her a topic before she asked, "So you been here a long time huh?"

"Uh, huh."

She wasn't having any luck locating a conversation button but that didn't bother her. After two months with a speechless quadriplegic as a roommate, she had become quite adept at one-sided conversations. "Amelia and I came here together," she offered. "She was in a bad car accident that left her paralyzed, I mean completely paralyzed. She couldn't talk, couldn't eat. All she could do was breathe." Kimmy recounted the entire tale in detail, leaving out very little. Twenty minutes into her story, she wondered if Charlie had fallen asleep. "Charlie, do you think I'm going to go to hell for killing Amelia?"

No response came and after a very long moment she decided he was indeed asleep. As she was pushing off from the chair to leave the room, he said, "The way I understand it, it wasn't murder. She told you to do it; you just did for her what her body couldn't. I think you'll be ok kid."

His youthful body held what Kimmy regarded as an old and wise soul, in his many years at the Harger Blish he had certainly seen a lot of judgments pass so his words gave her comfort.

She settled back into the chair with a lighter heart. "Do you have any kids?" she asked. That was his button. Charlie sat up in his bed and reached into his bedside nightstand producing a well-worn black leather trifold. His wife had filled it with family photos and buried him with it. It arrived at the Harger Blish the day of his funeral and it was his most prized and cherished possession. "That's Tom," he explained, "took a bad fall before this one was taken; fell out of a tree in the front yard and lost two teeth." A young, fair haired, toothless boy smiled back from the patina photo. Kimmy accepted and studied the picture. Next, Charlie proudly showed a photo of twin toddlers, girls dressed in frilly bottom bathing suites balancing tenuously on cherubic legs. "The twins weren't walking yet, you can see by their worried faces that they weren't too sure about standing either."

Accepting the second photo she asked, "How old were they?"

"Tommy was seven; Joanie and Judy were a bit more than a year. That one's Judy," he pointed to the picture, "with the ice cream stain on her suit." He smiled and shook his head thoughtfully. "Even today that girl is about as graceful as a fresh foal." It was the first time

Kimmy had seen him smile. "She's got a little girl just like her now too. Skeeter's always falling down or tripping over sidewalk goblins. Well, she's not so little anymore, I guess my grandbaby would be about your age now."

In astonished silence she pondered the fact that this fresh looking young man in front of her could have been her own grandfather. "Charlie, how long *have* you been here?"

His eyes traveled the ceiling as he search for the answer. "The girls were just about two when I died and they turned forty-three this past December so...." He didn't finish the sentence.

"I look out for the kids, I do what I can, give advice, warn them about life's dangers. Although they don't always heed my advice, I think they hear me."

"How long you plan to be here?"

"I first thought just long enough to say goodbye to Helen. Help her get over the grief. After about a year she hooked up with Stan. I figured she was moving on, so should I. Then the son of a bitch started smacking Tommy around. I wanted to kick his ass so bad. I just couldn't leave the kids with a bastard like that in the house. After a few years he moved on to a younger woman and was out of the picture. By then I was used to having the kids around and I liked watching them grow."

"So, they're grown and doing fine right?" she asked. "So why are you still here?"

"Helen asked me that. She was through here about five years ago; breast cancer. She stuck around for a couple of weeks before I walked her to the ferry. I almost got on but my feet were trembling and my heart was pounding so hard I could hear it beating in my ears. I know that sounds funny. Technically we don't even have a heart beat but I swear I could hear it." That was another realization that slapped Kimmy in the face. Slowly and inconspicuously she reached her hand to her chest for confirmation.

"Besides," he continued "this is my home; I've been here longer than I was alive. It's familiar. I like to visit my kids but I don't spend as much time with the grandkids as I did when they were little. Their music hurts my ears and their friends are a strange bunch. Kids these days are just a bit too selfish and ill-mannered if you ask me. No offense." He offered, realizing he was talking about Kimmy's generation. With a brief hesitation he interjected, "*and* I like the track. Bet they don't have that in heaven. I go most nights that I get out in body. Sure was glad to see Des Moines get the ponies. I bit the dust at Aksarben. Fifteen horses trampled me into the mud that day."

It wasn't a stretch to imagine Charlie on a race horse. He had the build and the gentle stern demeanor she'd have expected in a jockey. Kimmy put forth her own theory. "The way I picture heaven, you get to do exactly what you love to do and as much as you want to do it. If you want to ride those ponies instead of betting them, you should go on to heaven."

167

Racing hadn't entered his mind for a long time; it gave him pause for thought.

"Charlie," she said firmly, "your family is going to beat you to heaven if you don't put this world behind you. You've obviously lived a good life or you wouldn't have gotten the golden ticket. Go collect your deserved winnings."

Charlie lay back on the bed, hands clasped behind his head and with a heavy sigh he closed his eyes. It was a nonverbal cue that Kimmy understood. She placed the photos back on his bedside stand and headed for the door.

"I'll think on it," Charlie said. He sounded sincere and she smiled hoping that she had opened the door to his passage ever so slightly.

PART TWO

10

The old building brought forth memories of long ago Sunday morning church when, as a young boy, he sat wedged between the warm plump features of his grandmother and the contrasting erect, maple pews. While the pastor's words drifted into the background becoming occasional whispers of distant conversation, he intently studied the dancing dust on heavenly rays of light.

The sun soaked bricks of the structure had warmed one side of his body while the other side strained against the cool steel door which momentarily confined him. Dirk used a crow bar to pry a rear entrance door on the Harger Blish. Entry was made more difficult by debris piled from within. After a few shoulder plows he had managed to mine a two foot space. Cautiously, he viewed the interior of the old building before pushing through the obstruction. Long fingers of sunbeams reached into the dark room through upper windows while decades of dust danced in the light of the shadowed and silent structure. From somewhere within there were low murmurs of indiscernible conversation. Dirk slid the door closed behind him to hide obvious evidence of entry should the police make another drive by. Activity had slowed over the two weeks since the corpse was discovered; even the caution tape had been removed.

He moved as furtively as his prosthetic would allow; the crow bar up and ready for whatever he might encounter.

***

The lights blazed anew and the halls bustled with guests eager to socialize with others who had been similarly sealed away in their rooms as a precaution to limit human contact while investigators searched all corners of the building. The lockdown had been lifted just a few hours earlier and already the lobby was a flurry of activity. Two weeks of reflection on the frailty and sanctity of the soul combined with ample out of body indiscrete visits, had spurred a mass exodus of occupants. Dozens awaited the train that would transport them to the ferry and on to the final destination. However, activity ceased abruptly.

"Please return to your rooms calmly and quickly, the Seer is attempting to enter the building. Again, please return calmly, quickly and quietly to your quarters." The directive boomed above the crowd as if from a concealed speaker system.

Kimmy and Amelia had been in the dining hall laying out plans for an evening out with Charlie and Alex. Darkness was only a few hours away and they were anxious for the opportunity to stretch their legs. Kimmy didn't hesitate when the announcement came she abruptly stood and grabbed her friend's wrist. She had come face to face with this man and did not want a repeat encounter. Amelia shot a pleading look to Alex before she disappeared through the doorway. Evron Brown silently encouraged rapid progress of the guests as he ushered them down the dimmed halls. Kimmy was nearly at a run with Amelia in tow when Evron stepped quietly in front of her. With two down turned palms he pulsed slowly toward the floor, motioning the girls to slow. The halls had nearly emptied now. Quiet clicks repeated throughout the building as doors softly closed.

The girls had almost reached their door when a flashlight beam zipped by from behind. Terrified that they had been discovered they turned slowly with captured breath to see that the saber of light had pierced Evron's torso where he stood. Behind him several feet was the light wielding Seer, Dirk Cooper.

Quickly the light shot down the hall in the opposite direction as Dirk searched the dark passage for the source of faint mechanical clicks. When his thump, thud indicated his retreat, Evron nodded the girls to continue to their rooms and he turned in pursuit of Dirk. The girls didn't move, but watched in disbelief as Evron closed on the intruder.

With the door slightly ajar Charlie and Alex watched the scene unfold as Dirk approached their end of the hallway, flashlight jerking with his every awkward step. They saw Evron's steady and purposeful approach, eye's narrowed, jaw clenched. It wasn't difficult to interpret his intent – he meant contact and revenge.

Evron's job in the afterlife was that of gate keeper – the safety of the occupants of the Harger Blish was his primary responsibility. This mortal man before him had already ended one life and two souls. "Dirk" he said with a venomous growl. Dirk Cooper spun around wide-eyed at the sound of his name, his flashlight zipping into doorways and corners looking for the source. The two were just a few feet away from Alex and Charlie's open door. It was crazy; if Evron made contact with Dirk intentionally he would break a cardinal rule of engagement and pay a heavy price in servitude.

"You distract him," he said to Charlie, "I'll get Evron." Charlie understood and ran from the room to the opposite wall creating a breeze in the hall that chilled Dirk instantly so that he swung around to investigate. Charlie moved further down the hall and stomped loudly. Dirk heard the distant sound of muffled footsteps and went down the hall to investigate. As Evron prepared to follow, Alex grabbed his arm and Charlie who had quietly doubled back, pushed from behind simultaneously to bring the big man into their room. Evron recognized their honorable efforts and submitted.

Were his heightened senses and the creeks of an old building playing tricks on him? Dirk was nearly certain that this place was somehow associated with the corpse he had destroyed. He had heard voices and noises and his own name called but hadn't seen a thing. Although he wanted to stay and investigate further, the light was growing dim as the afternoon sun receded. Within minutes the place would be dark and he didn't want to navigate the debris with just a flashlight. Releasing an exasperated breath he bellowed to the exposed rafters, "You're here, I know you're here! Evron Brown, Kimberly Shobek." Kimmy's hand gripped Amelia's tightly as the Seer spoke her name. "And how about that girl you murdered, Amelia Spector, are you here too? There are more here, I can feel you even though I can't see you. I know you're here." His voice boomed louder in anger and frustration. "I consider it my mission to protect the people you are here to haunt and I will find a way to take you out of this world!" With that, he clambered back from where he came.

Inside the guy's small room Alex and Charlie looked to Evron for direction. But words of comfort were not the big man's strong suit. "Why are you two still here?! Your passage is set, take your tickets before you do something else stupid and lose your very souls," he rumbled.

"I can't leave without her." Alex said it out loud and it was a fact as plain as the earth and sky. "I love her and I will wait as long as I have to."

"When will we know their fates?" Charlie asked.

"You've been here longer than I have Charlie, you know everyone's situation is different and judgments vary case by case. Millions of people die every day on this earth. Some fates take longer to deliberate than others. I heard that once a guy was here for more than a year and when his sentence came he went to hell." He saw Alex's fearful face and offered an addendum, "I only heard one case like that, usually, you make it this far, you're going to the big house … eventually. You'll know when we all know."

Alex ran his fingers through his black curls and yanked on a handful with a frustrated growl. To which Evron responded, "It's called limbo kid – we just wait and see."

PART TWO

11

When the all-clear sounded an announcement followed, "All guests of the Harger Blish are required to attend this evening's meeting at 10PM. This excludes guests with registered departure plans. If you have filed your departure plan and received your ferry ticket, we wish you happiness and renewal when you arrive at your final destination." The announcement meant that external plans were canceled. With the number of guests leaving and no new arrivals, things were going to be pretty slow. New arrivals had been rerouted to the Omaha facility as a precaution. The only guests that would remain would be the handful who had taken up permanent residence and those awaiting judgment.

Again the man in the small brown bolo stood before a small crowd illuminated by the pale yellow spotlight and spoke in his standard nasal monotone. "As stated previously, the destruction of a soul is permanent. Although you will not be prohibited from leaving the Harger Blish in body, you are urged to use caution; avoid contact with the Seer at all costs. Your vessel is precious. Any damage has the potential to extinguish your soul."

"Regrettably, the Harger Blish has been slated for closure as soon as all pending judgments have been declared. The judgment council has agreed to review the guests in this facility with priority so decisions will be imminent. Upon closing, staff will be relocated to other nearby facilities."

Judgment, closure, departure, relocation; the words were unsettling to everyone in the room for their own reasons. Alex supportively looped his left arm around the crook of Amelia's elbow while he obscurely worked the individual knuckles of his right. "If she was sentenced to purgatory where would he wait?" he wondered.

Kimmy clasped Amelia's left hand so tightly that the discomfort distracted Amelia's own pensiveness.

Charlie's voice broke the hush that had befallen the auditorium. "What if we don't want to leave? This is my home. My family is in Des Moines." Murmurs of agreement rumbled throughout the auditorium.

"We understand that some of you have been reluctant to accept your granted passage," the small bolo'ed man responded, "and again we implore you to do so. It is a place for rejuvenation and it is your reward for living a beneficial and gracious life. However, you are not required, but requested to relocate. If you chose to remain at the Harger Blish it will be without guidance. The appearance of this dwelling will remain the same for you, absent of staff and amenities of course. However this structure will no longer be under the preservation society's protection and may be occupied or demolished. If it is demolished, you will need to move on to another dwelling. You have exactly one week. The last train departs Saturday at 8PM."

Again the little man disappeared with the dimming stage lights and the occupants filed out of the Harger Blish auditorium one final time.

"I gotta take it in one more time, breathe in that packing plant aroma, kick up the carp in the Raccoon river, listen to the midnight musicians at capitol hill. You guys wanna head out tomorrow night?" Kimmy's voice was unusually melancholy and somewhat pleading.

Amelia picked up Kimmy's usual persona and cheerily said, "I'm with ya Kimmy, let's say goodbye to Des Moines the right way."

"I'm bringing beer," Alex added. "I know the alcohol has no effect, but none of those things sound right without a six pack."

They smiled and looked to Charlie for a response. He lightly touched a shiny gold ticket that peeked out of his pocket. "I scheduled my trip," he confessed. "Guess it's time." Kimmy teared up behind her smile and hugged Charlie's neck. He patted her back with some reserved distance. Although he appreciated her happiness, emotional displays made him uncomfortable. When she released him he continued, "But I do want to make one last trip to see my boy, smell the track, just say goodbye."

"You made the right choice," Alex said with an extended hand. "I'll see you on the streets; I hear they're covered in gold."

"I hope they're covered in horse shit." Charlie responded with a wink in Kimmy's direction. Amelia kissed his cheek and he squeezed both girls' hands as he assured them, "I'll see you all there."

***

Mary Shobek scrubbed the already sparkling kitchen floor on her hands and knees sliding a bucket of soapy water with her as she crawled. "I don't know if or when I'll see you again mom." Kimmy's voice didn't startle the woman nor did it stop her work.

"Hi, baby," she replied.

"I don't know how it works." Kimmy stood inside the doorway not wanting to soil the still wet tile. "When you get your marching orders what happens next? Ya know," she hesitated, "Let's just say the order is some sort of service like you're doing."

"You leave the Harger Blish immediately upon receiving judgment. You board a train for an education facility where you learn your job and your requirements. Someday a facilitator will come to you and declare your service is done and you can go on. Don't know when that will happen for me; I'm still waiting." Mary stopped scrubbing, she stood up and strolled across the wet floor. Soapy suds dripped from the yellow rubber gloves that soaked Kimmy's shoulders when her mother pulled her in close for a hug.

"Don't you worry baby, you're a good girl. I'll see you again." She kissed the top of Kimmy's head, smiled reassuringly, then returned to her task.

PART TWO

12

Clutching the styrofoam16 oz steaming cup of Hardee's coffee like it was the last life giving sustenance on earth, Laurie addressed her team. Her temples throbbed from the thunderous beat down the chief had laid on her moments ago.

"Please tell me we have something to go on," she pleaded. One by one the detectives relayed their futile findings. The letters Po were the mark of Porcelain Plus, a distributor out of Omaha which supplied most of the diners in the Midwest with dishes. The Harger Blish was clean, no forced entry, no evidence of squatters, not even tracks in the dust. Every square yard of Glendale had been walked and, except for a few toppled headstones and some mausoleum graffiti, the place was undisturbed.

She sighed hard, released her coffee cup and rubbed her pounding forehead. "DCI reported the lab found nothing suspect in the caskets." There was a moment of silence when she realized someone was missing.

From the doorway Tom spoke through the dredges of a jelly filled donut. "Carla's scrubs were hospital issue; had Mercy's perma-stamp on them. Those clothes could have been lifted from anywhere. My 15 year old son's got a pair; said a friend of a friend lifted them from a garment closet. I didn't push the issue of stolen goods because we'd have to run in a third of East High's sophomore's. They aren't exactly a hard item to come by. Somebody ought to talk to Mercy about locks for their closet doors." He popped the last of the confection into his mouth and sat in an open chair dusting powdered sugar from his tie.

"What about victim two? Any word on Mr. Kim's clothes?" she asked.

"Now there's a weird one," Tom continued. "No labels of any sort, not even evidence of labels. Usually there are pieces of label embedded in a seam if someone tears them out. Industrial clothing makers over sew in an area where a label would go; not with this guy's clothes, not even the freakin shoes had a marker. The lab is still going over them looking for a "common thread" so to speak. But at this point we ain't got shit to go on."

PART TWO

13

A rumbling underfoot, barely audible, signaled the train's departure. The once bustling establishment was both literally and figuratively becoming a ghost town. "This place is really creeping me out," Kimmy admitted as she and Amelia entered the vast and empty lobby. "How scary does a place have to be to freak out a ghost?" Kimmy quipped in a predictable attempt to lighten the moment.

Amelia glanced at the grandfather clock that guarded their usual exit. Straight up 10:00. The clock did not bong, it never had; but at the moment that it should, she jumped with fright as Alex tapped her shoulder.

"Wow, a bit jumpy?" he asked.

"Kimmy's right, this place is getting creepy." Amelia's tension summarily dispersed with Alex's presence. Even in unremarkable clothes he looked remarkable she noticed. "Did Charlie get off?"

"He was gone before I woke up from my visit with Grandma." The trio headed for the door. With no sign of Mr. Brown to issue warnings or wisdom, they pushed through to the outside into a springtime starry night. Late April in Iowa could bring any weather. On this night it was brisk but not cold, invigorating without shivering.

"I wanna stop at the Get N Go to pick up some snacks. Ya wanna head to the river or the Capitol first?" Kimmy wasn't hungry but it was a familiar pattern she'd followed on nights like this with her friends on life's other side.

In brown paper bags each carried their favorite junk food and beverage as they headed up Grand toward the State Capitol Building and the historic park monuments that surround it. Musicians were often found there on pleasant nights sharing their art with anyone who wanted to listen. The night felt right, fond memories were shared. In their laughter they were oblivious to his approach.

Kimmy's jacket was scruffed tightly about her neck. A .45 caliber dug into her rib cage. "Hello Kimberly," Dirk snarled. Alex and Amelia froze where they stood. "And you are Amelia. I don't know you... yet," he spoke looking at Alex, "but I'll ID you later; or maybe I'll just wait for the paper to post your name when they discover your rotting corpse with these two."

"Move down that alley very slowly." He motioned with his head toward a narrow dark drive that ran next to Capital City Florist. It was an error in judgment; the poorly lit alley was not to his advantage. He didn't see the watery pothole before he sunk his prosthesis into the puddle. With an awkward lurch the gun tumbled from his hand landing with a splash in the murky hole.

Pulling out of her coat, Kimmy and the others sprinted into the darkness. It wasn't a through street but a parking lot closed off by surrounding buildings. With no exit or retreat they anxiously tried doors. Alex laid his shoulder into one that seemed to give. "Here!" he yelled to the girls. They all rammed the door together. A shot rang out just as they crashed through the door.

Dirk watched the three spill into the flower shop and heard the shrill wail of the security alarm.

Again from the shadows Dirk watched the events unfold. Two black and whites were on the scene in minutes. Three figures were placed into squad cars and escorted away. He had hoped that they would run out the front door making for easy targets to be picked off. That would have made a sensational headline tomorrow he thought. But he realized the kids knew they stood a better chance with the cops than with him.

He didn't know where the bus was headed but was glad to be out of the cop's line of sight. It passed several stops. The one Dirk chose to exit served liquor and just happened to be the race track.

***

He dabbed the mint flavored Colgate onto his index finger and crammed the paste up his right then left nostril causing his eyes to water fiercely and his nose to ignite. Although extremely uncomfortable, at least Alex could no longer smell the vomit that his cellmate spewed about the tiny room. The drunk had felt better following the upheaval and passed out on a very nearby cot. While on lock down at the Harger Blish he'd had ample time to contemplate what the future held for him, to speculate on the heaven that awaited. Now he contemplated a more immediate scenario. In the cell directly across the hall Jane Doe One and Jane Doe Two pondered the situation in silence. Amelia reviewed in her mind the chapter of The Book that warned of the dangers of light exposure as she stared up at the skylight in the hall between the two cells.

The Book explained; *it is not the sun which degrades the cellular structure of a post life entity rather the magnetic and electrical interference which increases during daylight hours.*

185

The earth is covered by a fluctuating membrane, the atmosphere, which is constantly being bombarded by strong solar winds. During the day, this membrane is at its most dense. However, at night, when sheltered from the sun, the barrier extends much farther into space and has much less tension. In the same way that television and radio reception improves at night, postlife entities can effectively manifest because there is less magnetic and electrical resistance. When the cellular structure is no longer viable an entity's tangible form will dissolve. The unconscious entity will reestablish in the sanctity of the designated safe house when adequate time has passed for the entity's cellular rejuvenation, a process that will vary in duration but is typically complete in forty-eight hours. The exceptions, of course, are pergatories whose designated duties require daytime activities.

Kimmy wondered how this incident would impact their final judgment which was probably days away. Neither she nor Amelia spoke. They hadn't said one word, not to each other and not to authorities. It had been approximately four hours since they were captured inside the flower shop. She revisited the scene in her mind...

"On the ground, hands behind your head," the officer had commanded over the shrill scream of the alarm. All three reacted immediately knowing that any abrasion could be a soul ending event. The three lay face down in close proximity. When the alarm finally stopped Amelia had whispered to the others, "Say nothing, not one single word to anyone, we'll be out of this by daylight." They had been taken into custody for breaking and entering, placed into the back of two squad cars and transported to the Polk county jail. Amelia, Kimmy and Alex hadn't made eye contact with the officers, hadn't respond to questions. Except when absolutely necessary they had stared at the floor.

A black ink roller traversed all five fingers on the right hand and prints were made; first the thumb, then each successive finger, then a four finger drop. The process had been repeated on the left hand. They were photographed and left alone in a small, windowless white room. A wood laminate folding table and six metal folding chairs had been the room's only dressing.

There they sat for what must have been two hours by Kimmy's calculations. She had counted seconds to pass the time. Occasionally officers had re-entered to ask, "Are you ready to make a statement? If you give us your names things will go much easier." After two hours of assorted badgering attempts they had been placed in cells for the next shift to deal with.

She figured they were caught around 11:30, half hour in the car, two hours in the questioning room and two hours in their cell. It was probably around 4AM. They had two hours before the sun came up. It was a calculation Alex and Amelia had also completed.

"Don't want you fading away from us so quickly," the words of Evron Brown came back to Kimmy as on the morning of their arrival when he had warned her and Amelia about the dangers of going out into the light. What had that meant – fading away from us? Kimmy hadn't read that chapter.

***

As luck would have it, his son tumbled to the floor directly in front of him. He had bent to retrieve a winning ticket on the final race of the night and was bumped from behind by an off kiltered patron. Charlie offered his hand. "Thanks buddy," the man said as he took the extended hand which helped him to his feet.

Charlie held his son's hand for a moment before he said, "Good luck, I hope life treats you well. Good bye."

The man eyed Charlie with a friendly but perplexed smile and said, "Thanks, the same to you."

It was shortly after midnight when Charlie left the track for the last time.

***

Dust danced in the sunlight that filtered down through the ceiling window and shined warmly on the cot where John Doe should have been. A second guard was opening the locked but empty cell of Jane's one and two.

PART TWO

14

"What the Fuck?" the captain kicked over a trash can spilling the contents, which included a half full cup of stale coffee, onto the floor. "How can three kids just disappear?"

"There was a guy in here about 2AM asking if he could post bail for three kids who had been picked up near East 6th and Walnut. He didn't know their names and frankly he seemed a little drunk. I'd just come on duty and had no idea who he was talking about. The young field training officer (FTO) was obviously unnerved and anxious; a latent stutter emerged. "He… He… He wa-walked with kind of a clumsy limp. B-B-Banged his right leg on a door p-pretty hard on his way out and didn't even wince. I think it was a f-f-f-fake leg. P-Probably mid-forties, big guy, l-lots of sc-sc-sc-sc-scars and a really mean looking pink scar that went from the middle of his left arm up into his sleeve." He took a deep breath and focused on the shiny diamond chip on the captain's tie clip. "Guy smelled like Jack Daniels. I should have had someone put him in dry dock but he wasn't causing a fuss."

"I don't want any of this information leaving this fucking room! Not a word of it gets leaked or I'll put every one of you on probation! This is a GOD DAMNED disgrace." He addressed the FTO, "Bring me the report and wipe the "Doe's" out of the log. I'll handle this myself," he grumbled. The officer scrambled rapidly out the door to the book while the Captain continued his rant to all who were present and had contact with, or responsibility for, the perpetrators. "Can't trust a one of you fuckin fuck ups to track these kids down! How in THE FUCK?" he bellowed as he slammed the conference room door behind him.

With the scrubbed duty log in hand he paced the floor of his office mumbling to himself. Finally, he took a deep breath before gathering the Does' files and exited into the mid-morning light that filled the hall from the skylights above.

Officer Todd Rounds was filling his water bottle at the fountain when the captain growled menacingly, "Rounds, we need to talk." Todd followed the captain into his office. "You've wanted to make detective for some time now and I think I can get you there if you can help me out with something." He explained the details he had on the missing kids' case.

"I need this done quietly. I'm the only one who gets to see the report. You can't share this information, especially not with Laurie. You understand?" He did, but he knew he would; they shared everything. "I'll fill your beat. This is your priority now. Your story, should anybody ask, is that I have you on a private surveillance; an uppity up with a peeping Tom. These are the videos from last night. Don't check them back in. Bring them directly to me."

Grey and white footage of the entry way showed the arresting officers enter with three youths, a male and two females. One female was absent a coat. There was nothing distinctive about the perpetrators. Todd scratched notes on a yellow lined notepad as he watched.

1. Where was the third perps coat? 2. Why did they not speak?

He fast forwarded to 2:10 AM. As officer had described, the suspected accomplice limped clumsily, his right leg obviously a prosthetic, was still a relatively new apparatus for him.

3. Check area hospitals for recent amputations and right leg prosthesis.

As the suspect turned to leave there was an excellent face shot. He paused the tape and stared. Something very familiar but couldn't place him. The report said the cells were checked at 3AM and the perps were still there. Todd forwarded the tape to 2:59 and watched the next three hours of footage to see if the kids went out the front door unnoticed. There were two separate DUIs admitted but no other activity at all.

Pondering the building's access points he recalled multiple exits, most alarmed and only used when the fire safety tested them. The only other building exit which was not alarmed, besides the main entry, was called the dog door; the entrance all officers and staff used to enter and exit the building. It opened into the secured parking garage. A code was required for both entering and exiting the facility. More and more this was starting to feel like an inside job. An officer had to open the cells, would give them the code would need to time it right and be very quiet about it.

4. Who was on duty? What was the motive?

Laurie entered carrying two brown bags of groceries. "Hey what are you doing home?"

"The official story I'm supposed to tell you is that I'm doing surveillance of an uppity up's house for a peeper."

"And the unofficial story?" She was intrigued.

"You gotta keep this one under your hat or you'll be supporting me while I look for a new job." He told her the story as he helped her unpack the groceries. While he recounted the events and stocked the cold items into the refrigerator, Laurie reached into the remaining sack and stuffed a small box in her sweater pocket. Then she continued unpacking the goods.

Todd opened the new peanut butter and plunged his finger into the center of the jar extracting a glob. "So if it's an inside job, I can't figure out where this limping character fits in." He said before sucking the nutty paste from his finger. They went through several jars of Jiff a month. Sometimes Todd finished off a jar with a spoon while watching a movie.

Laurie headed for the television. "I know that face too. Tom's got a pencil drawing of him pinned to his bulletin board. He looks really pissed off in Tom's drawing but I'm sure it's the same guy."

She headed for the bathroom while Todd pondered the coincidence that the kids had been arrested in the floral shop where Tom's wife worked. He added to his notes:

5. Check on Tom's whereabouts last night.

He wondered how he would do that without looking suspicious. Talking around a mouth of peanut butter he asked Laurie through the bathroom door, "Can you ask Tom where he got that picture and what he did last night – you know in casual conversation?" There was no response and he heard the water running in the sink. He opened the door and caught her washing her hands. He repeated his question and she answered but her response was rattled and nervous. He saw the EPT.

Eyes wide, his agape jaw grew into a smile…. "Is there a chance?"

"Not likely," she said somewhat hopeful. "I know….. every fertility specialist has told me it would take a miracle, but I've never been this late before so I thought I'd check. Sorry didn't want to dash your hopes too."

"Can we check?"

"Fifteen seconds." Time crawled by. "It's negative."

Todd smiled to lift her spirits although his were deflated too. "Wanna try again?" They fell into bed with the open jar of Jiff.

In the post-coital position, Todd stroked her hair and took in the smell of Suave Apple Blossom. The phone rang, both reached for it on the bedside table. Laurie answered.

She hung up and rolled over to Todd propped on an elbow with a perplexed look. "Seriously, why is it that lately, every time we have sex I get a dead body phone call?"

"Serial?"

"Looks like it."

He followed her naked backside with his eyes until the bathroom door closed. He heard the shower and drifted off to sleep.

PART TWO

15

It was a sleep that lasted four days; nightmares, fantasies, fiction and reality, future, past and present; a continual stream of subconscious episodes. The worst were the nightmares.

Clear cool spring water splashed over his naked torso when Amelia popped up from the deep quarry waters in front of him; her honey colored hair wet and long on her bare shoulders. She wrapped her arms around his neck and pulled her round and chilled breasts into his warm chest. The heat of their two bodies cocooned them. In a swimming embrace they tenderly kissed, inhaled each other's breath and lingered wanting more, searching each other's eyes for love. Alex drew a slow breath to gather himself with the courage to utter the words he'd never spoken to her, "I love you," when Amelia was ripped away from him violently.

Like a person shark bitten, her eyes wide with terror, she searched the water beneath her for the injurious intruder. Another violent tug whisked her several yards away from Alex. She swallowed a lung full of water, coughed, spit and screamed Alex's name. Swimming as hard as ever he had before, trying to reach her, he found himself elevated from the water. A bright beam of light had suspended him where the clouds parted. The beam was warm and soft like a pillow of cotton surrounding him but he resisted it's comfort and writhed with all his strength to break free. Amelia screamed his name again before finally she was dragged down into the quarry depths.

"No! Take me with you, I'll go with you. Don't leave!!!" he cried out in heart wrenching pain.

Typically, in dreamland, your body will awaken you when panic sets in and your heart rate soars, but for Alex, Amelia and Kimmy no dream would end until they had fully re-established their form.

***

"God judges His children today by evaluating how well they have lived and how well they have died. Their rewards in God's Kingdom will depend on their character development during and after their mortal life. It is a process requiring time and opportunity for learning and growth. Judgment day has come." The hallowed voice echoed throughout the bright white room.

Two heavy wooden chairs with red velvet cushions were positioned center stage facing a committee obscured in misty fog, only outlines of forms were visible. Amelia and Kimmy each occupied a chair. Alex stood defiantly erect behind Amelia's right shoulder.

"This court will hear the case of Alex William Garreth," a commanding voice announced. A gavel echoed loudly through the room. The girls had been ready to accept their fate but Alex's was predetermined. With utter shock they stared at Alex. He didn't look surprised.

"You have broken the rules of engagement with the mortal world, you have disobeyed the doctrine of The Book, exposed the existence of afterlife. As promised, your consequence will be immediate and severe. You shall suffer the vengeance of eternal fire…as shall you, Kimberly Shobek and you, Amelia Spector.

"No!" Amelia sprang from her chair. "He has his ticket. The Ferry has been waiting for him since the moment he got here!" She attacked the wall of white; repelled like a magnet from a like charge, she could not penetrate the fog.

Her loud fervent plea fell on deaf ears as the forms slowly faded from view. "Please, Alex is a good person. He stayed for me." She dropped to her knees before the veil and sobbed, "Please let him go to heaven. It's my fault he stayed." Her shoulders shook and sobs came with rasping breaths. "Please," she whimpered helplessly between sobs, "please."

***

The sky turned pink through the frosted glass in the ceiling just beyond the barred door. Kimmy watched as Amelia faded into the olive green wool blanket atop which she lay. Her own wool blanket pricked her back and legs as each protruding fiber became a searing hot needle branding her immobile corps with smoldering black dots of sizzling flesh. Dozens of charred black hands clawed through the smoldering cloth and dragged Kimmy through the cot and down into the foul smelling, blazing hot, nauseating tunnel of torture which most certainly led to hell. None of the pain she endured was as painful as the realization that she was doomed to eternity in hell. She had failed her God, her family and her friends and that failure tortured her more than anything. Sobbing between screams she cried out, "No....!

No…! Let me try again. I'll do whatever you need me to do. Please let me show you I am a good person."

Cyclists pedaled quickly past on a beautiful spring morning. Teens held hands and strolled through the lush green grass while she watched motionless behind an invisible barrier with flames spitting at her backside, immobilized for all time in her wheel chair watching life race past.

Amelia, Alex and Evron hovered above Kimmy coaxing her quietly out of her nightmare. She sweat profusely and winced with painful jerks and gyrations then slowly opened her tear-filled eyes to thankfully find familiar faces above her.

"Are we in Heaven?"

Alex responded, "We're in the Harger."

She blew out a heavy puff of relief that dramatically inflated her cheeks. When she wiped the sweat from her brow with her sleeve she noticed her nails were longer as were those of Alex and Amelia.

Overwhelming weakness possessed her body and with great effort she pushed herself to a sitting position. "This may be as close to heaven as I get and I've never been so happy to be dead in all my life." She smiled widely then noticed that none smiled back. Apprehensively she asked, "What's wrong?"

Evron spoke. "The seer has taken another. Charlie never made it to the ferry."

Terror, jubilation and tragedy were all processed in the span of only a few moments, overriding her ability to respond. In stunned silence she chewed absently on her upper lip, perhaps to keep it from quivering. No one spoke for a long moment.

"He was going," Kimmy finally said, "It was finally his time. What are we gonna do?" She was looking for a solution to bring Charlie back, her mind refusing to process the loss.

"We stop him," said Evron flatly and firmly, referring to Dirk. "The Harger is gone in three days. I have three days to stop him." Evron turned abruptly and exited the room.

With some guilt for thinking not of Charlie, Amelia said, "We have three days until judgment". Kimmy fell back onto her sweat soaked bed and covered her face with her pillow.

Alex wrapped his arms protectively around Amelia.

PART THREE

1

Detective Tom Hawthorne kept his desk and office space much the same as he had kept his bachelor apartment, when he was a bachelor; three layers of filth each more disgusting than the next. On the surface was yesterday's trash, a Styrofoam cup containing a swig of coffee and yesterday's ham sandwich, the crust hardened but edible in a pinch. The Styrofoam cup occupied another Styrofoam cup and yet another; stacked like little Russian tea dolls. Each held another swig of unsipped, stale, then molded coffee.

He was about to add another level to the teetering tower with a snack sized bag of partially eaten Highland potato chips, when Laurie entered the room. She was revolted but tolerant to an extent, surmising that this was a defiant and desperate grasp at misplaced masculine independence, Susan would have never let him live like that at home. Only because she was working an angle did she suppress the urge to deal with his offensive office hygiene. "Hey, you and Susan were out late Tuesday Night. I saw you guys in the bar at Cabo's around midnight. But you were gone before I could make my way over to say hi," she lied.

"We weren't at Cabo's. MacGyver is on Tuesday nights. We don't leave the house on MacGyver night."

She knew that was true, MacGyver was Tom's water cooler topic. He recounted the episode every Wednesday morning with other show addicts in the station. She made a mental note to call Todd with the news. "God, I could have sworn it was you guys." She continued to cover while she crossed nonchalantly to Tom's bulletin board. "Hey, I've been meaning to ask, who is this pencil drawing of?"

"Don't know. I kicked it up in the dust when I was doing a poke around the Harger Blish. It's pretty intense don't ya think. There's no artist mark but whoever drew it is pretty damn good." Tom was not at all suspicious and inquired about the file Laurie held. "Is that the file on the new stiff?"

"More like a file on the ancient artifact. Lab results show the skeleton is at least forty years post mortem."

"That's an odd twist. I don't even know if we have dentals that go back that far. Gonna be tough to ID that one."

A phone call interrupted their conversation. Laurie responded to the caller, "We're not at a dead end so to speak… if you recall the last three vics were all from Glenndale. I've got a couple of guys there with the grounds keeper now. They'll comb the markers from 1940 to 1945 to check for disturbance. Yes – I'm aware we'll need family consent to exhume. I'll deal with that... Thanks for the kind offer Drake but I don't need DCI's assistance at this time."

Tom covered his mouth to conceal the noise that shook his shoulders with amusement.

When she hung up the phone she grunted "UGH!" then beat herself twice in the forehead with the file folder she held. "Call me if you get any news," she said before leaving the office in search of Todd.

Laurie perched on the side of Todd's desk; his was tidy and orderly, a nearly empty in box and an out box with color coded file folders not a paper askew. He was obsessed with Acco fasteners. She filled him in on Tom's whereabouts and the drawing.

"I'll casually bump into Susan and verify the story. Thanks. I'd have hated for him to be involved but I sure would like a lead somewhere." The phone rang. Mercy Hospital reported a short list of amputees dating back six to twelve months; one fit the bill: caucasian, male, forty, left leg amputee.

While Todd continued his conversation, Laurie slipped out the door waiving silently as she left. He entered Stephen D. Cooper into the DSM PD Data base and found a short record of misdemeanors: public intox, trespassing, assault and most recently a speeding ticket with a date matching the amputation. Address in hand, he wasted no time.

Capital City Florist was on the way to Mr. Cooper's house. He stopped in and was greeted by the friendly and familiar face of Susan Hawthorn. "Hey Susan, how are you?"

"Oh Todd, what a surprise! I haven't seen you and Laurie for too long." She was a genuine sweet heart; ever pleasant, the kind of person that listened and responded with obvious sincerity to any stranger's trivia. "Are you here on business or pleasure? You know we had a break in two nights ago."

"Yeah, I heard about that, everything ok?"

"Oh sure, we're fine, they didn't take a thing, not one thing."

Actually, I stopped by because we didn't get a chance to say hi to you at Cabo's Tuesday. We saw you in the bar about midnight but you and Tom were gone before we could make it over."

"Oh, you must have seen our evil twins," she chided. "Tuesday is MacGyver night don't ya know. We never miss it; and good golly I can't remember the last time I was in a bar or up past midnight for that matter."

Tom blushed with embarrassment realizing that his fable would have absolutely been out of character for Susan. Relieved that the story was confirmed he covered his fib by ordering a spring bouquet to be sent to Laurie at the Station. When he had paid and was about to leave, Susan asked, "What do you want the card to say?"

He hesitated, smiled wryly and said, "Choosy lovers choose Jiff."

Looking momentarily puzzled, her eyes widened and her cheeks flushed when finally she understood. "Ohhh, Todd Rounds you are so bad," she scolded.

***

The proximity of the train rattled his car while it idled on the gravel drive of the dilapidated relic of a residence in Des Moines's south east bottoms; an area of the city neglected in both cash and council by a municipality in denial. Dirk Cooper's residence was nearly on top of the tracks. Todd waited for the train to pass before he approached; knocking would have otherwise fallen on deaf ears.

Step clomp, the occupant approached the dusty screen door. "What do you need?" gruffed the man.

"Stephen Cooper?"

"Dirk." He responded flatly.

"Fine. But you are by birth Stephen Cooper right?" Todd pressed.

"Yeah, but it's Dirk."

"I'm Officer Todd Rounds. I've got a few questions for you – about three youths you were inquiring about two nights ago. Can I come in?"

He retreated from the doorway into the house. Todd thought he heard Dirk say, "Come on in," so he did.

"I didn't give them my name. How'd you find me?"

"You got a unique injury that makes you pretty easy track down. You can't get away with as much as you used to. Bet it's put a hitch in your fight profits too." He wanted to let Dirk know that he was aware of the character he was dealing with.

"Puts a hitch in a lot of things. So tell me about the kids, you still got'em?" He wondered how ghosts would hold up in captivity.

"How do you know them?" Todd avoided Dirk's question.

Before he responded Dirk thought about how his honest reply would be met. He slid onto the cracked vinyl of the circa 1960 rusted chrome kitchen chair and with his good leg he kicked a similar chair in Todd's direction.

A Lucky Strike filterless tumbled out of a soft-pack and he lit it with a long pull, giving him time to form a response, "I don't."

"Let me be blunt." Todd dropped a manila file folder squarely on the table stirring the ashes inside of the dingy, plaid, bean bag ash tray. He pulled three mug shots from the folder and lined them up in front of Dirk, "I need their names."

Staring back from the photographs were three faces Dirk didn't recognize; two females and a male, brown hair, round faces, vacant eyes. "These are not pictures of the kids *I* was looking for."

"Who were you looking for?"

Dirk had slept very little in the past few weeks and not at all in the past 48 hours. His late night encounter with the stiff at the race track still had him on edge. He recalled the way that the young man's head popped right off in his hands when he attempted to snatch him from behind. His intent was to interrogate not to decapitate. The body fell to the ground and the flesh powdered and vanished in his hands leaving him holding only a bleached skull.

"You all right, man?" Todd asked noticing the paleness and vacant stare.

Dirk was catatonic and pallid, sweat beaded on his brow and upper lip, his cigarette quivered dropping a long ash onto the table. The officer's words jolted Dirk back to the moment and he said, "No." After a long pause he continued, "Look, you're gonna think I'm a total fuckin' salted nut bar but I gotta tell someone. Those three kids you guys got are the living dead." Todd looked away and scratched his head. He wasn't pondering the living dead part of the sentence but the fact that the police no longer had them had entered his mind.

Recognition of the situation seemed to filter through Dirk's muddied mind and he said "You ain't got 'em anymore have ya? That's why you're here. You think they broke out and I might know where they are. They're ghosts man." He emphasized the word "ghosts" then recited the story withholding incriminating details...who was destroyed, where and how. The story had been headlines "Serial grave robber plays dress up with dead." He didn't want to be linked to that.

"The dead walk among us. I'm telling ya – when I had my accident I died. The doctors brought me back but I was really dead for a few minutes. I saw this guy that I knew was dead and he was standing beside me in line. I saw a couple others too, ones I didn't know. So now...I've been seeing these same people – these dead people here, just walking around like you and me. Problem is that I'm the only one who sees them for who they were before they died – to everyone else they look like some other person. Must be because I died too so I got the gift." He could tell he was losing Todd. "Now I ask myself, why would dead people be walking around and I figure they got a score to settle. They are probably here to screw with someone that pissed 'em off when they were alive, ya follow me?" Todd had dealt with nutcases before but if even the nutcrackers occasionally gave up pertinent details so he nodded and listened.

"Now these three you got here, I only know two of them; the guy I haven't ID'd yet. But these girls, they are the ones that got scraped out of that VW bug in Mercy's parking garage, the girl that killed her crippled roommate and then shot herself. I was at the hospital then learning how to walk on this damn thing." He thumped his prosthesis.

Todd had been the first on the scene for that discovery. He was at the hospital that day too with a crack case he'd caught robbing a 7-Eleven that morning. The image of the two girls still rattled his cage.

It was apparent the guy was either a great liar or truly psychotic. "I need to know where you went when you left the police station Monday night," he redirected.

Although the gamers at the track could verify his whereabouts he thought it better not to mention that location since the most recent corpse had already been found. "I came home and went to bed."

"Don't leave town, I might have some more questions for you." Todd stood to leave.

Feeling dismissed and still wanting to prove his case he offered "Check their fingernails. I don't know why, but dead people have these long thick yellow nails."

Todd looked at Dirk searching for a sign of sanity or a signature of deceit then he quietly continued toward the door.

"You don't have them anymore do you?"

He didn't halt his stride.

"You want to find 'em, I think I can help ya with the Shobek girl." Todd paused at the door waiting for some disclosure from his only suspect. "She's got a brother. I been tailing him to see if I could spot her. He hangs out at The Cave. I bet you could catch her there."

The screen door thwapped as Todd exited.

"You don't have them because they are ghosts man… they just disappeared," Dirk yelled out the door. He watched the unmarked LeBaron drive away.

PART THREE

2

"I want you to hop the next train and take the ferry," Amelia addressed Alex firmly. "Your taking too much of a risk being here. I'll meet you in a few days when my judgment is passed." She had very little faith that she would get an immediate ticket but attempted to make Alex believe her.

"Nice try," he acknowledged, "but I'm not leaving without you." He stared into her pleading brown eyes. "Look, I fell in love with you four years ago and only got to spend one night with you before I lost you. I'll be damned if I am going to lose you again." He leaned in and kissed her tear moistened lips. "You're stuck with me, for eternity."

She smiled and touched his chin, stubbly from the accelerated growth of three days. "You look like Jesus," she replied.

As Kimmy emerged from the bathroom sporting recently trimmed hair and nails, she responded to Amelia's remark "Then maybe *Jesus dos* is our "in" with the big guy." Kimmy's abrupt appearance interrupted an embrace. Feeling awkward, she dramatically threw herself against the wall and feigned illness.

"Ack –Ack," she wretched as if joking. "Would you two get a room? Oh, never mind, you have a room. I'll be going now." She smiled sincerely for her friend's happiness and backed out of the room.

***

"Mom, you here?" Kimmy's mother scrubbed the already sparkling kitchen floor on her hands and knees as she responded.

"Not much cookin' to do. Not many residents left. You want something to eat?" She asked.

"No." She watched her mother make small circular motions with a sponge, occasionally dipping it again into soapy water.

"I hear judgment comes in a few days. Looks like all of us will be gone from here on Friday. Is that why you've come?"

Kimmy wanted to make her mom feel better about the approaching deadline but couldn't find the words. "I just wanted to…. yeah, I suppose that's why. It's time for me to say goodbye." Her words were soft and worried.

"No," her mother responded nonchalantly, "just, see ya later. Don't you worry. You're a good girl. Maybe a little time scrubbing dishes or the like but you'll be just fine. I'll see you again child. You turned out just fine," she reassured her daughter, "you're one of the best things I ever did with my life; you and your brother," she scrubbed as she talked.

"Thanks mom." Kimmy got down on the floor next to her diligently working mother and hugged her, "I love you."

"I love you too baby." She patted Kimmy's arm then resumed her scrubbing. Tears streamed down Mary's cheek and mixed with the sponge and water as she worked.

***

It was nearly 11 PM when Kimmy left the Harger Blish. She knew it was risky but one more goodbye was in order.

Cautiously, she exited the building and moved quickly to the nearest bus stop; staying in the streetlights as much as possible. It had become obvious on the night of their capture that visible places were more desirable with Dirk on the prowl. He wouldn't strike in public.

Again inside the lascivious smoke filled establishment she found her brother alone at a table near the stage. This time Kimmy was there in body wanting only brief physical contact and an opportunity to *say* goodbye. She leaned against the bar devising a plan of approach. She couldn't just go up to him and ask to sit down; how awful it would be for her brother to think she was hitting on him.

Kimmy pulled up a chair at the empty table behind him when she realized that, oddly, three drinks sat before him; all full, only one with ice. He held the iced drink in his hand and turned it around and around as if admiring the beverage. He smelled it then cupped it again in his hands and stared vacantly at the stage but beyond the dancer. Kimmy also noticed an open pack of Marlboros; on the table three cigarettes lay stacked end to end like rail cars on a track. Three more were inside the ashtray broken in two but not smoked.

Jimmy's private thoughts were interrupted when an eager dancer knelt in front of him. She laid her tasseled double D's across the table in a column like a dish offered for serving. Her smoke stained grin asked for his approval. To the woman's surprise and to Kimmy's, Jimmy left the table, his drinks and his cigarettes and headed for the door. The dancer returned to the stage and Kimmy seized the opportunity. She quickly grabbed the pack from the table; catching up to her brother she tapped his shoulder. He turned to face her without a hint of recognition.

"You forgot your cigarettes," Kimmy said.

"No I didn't. I don't want em."

Kimmy smiled and extended her hand. Instinctive Jimmy reciprocated the greeting. She shook his hand with a big grin, "Goodbye."

"Bye."

When Jimmy had gone, she pondered the encounter again while she waited for an appropriate amount of time to pass before she could leave without seeming obvious. Not a drink, not a smoke! He was on his way to a healthier, hopefully happier, life.

The parking lot of The Cave was dimly lit, probably to protect the identities of the occupants. This should have given her cause for caution but Kimmy's heart was glowing with the realization of her brother's success. When she hopped a puddle with a jubilant bound Dirk stepped out of the shadows a few feet in front of her, a pistol at his side. Instantly, she turned to run but Todd stepped out of the shadows to halt her retreat.

"Halt, Police!" he yelled, recognizing her as one of the female jail break suspects and although she didn't recognize him at all she was glad to have a protective witness.

"It's her Rounds. It's Kimmy Shobek; I know she don't look like it to you."

Todd noticed the gun in Dirk's hand. "Drop the gun Cooper and you better have a permit for that." Dirk pointed the Glock 9mm at Kimmy. He still hadn't slept: almost three days without sleep. He was edgy, possessed by a goal and anxious to see it through. Todd raised his gun in response, "I said drop it Dirk," he barked.

Kimmy's head snapped quickly from gun point to gun point, her feet frozen in place. "*Holy Mary, Mother of God, pray for us sinners now, and at the hour of death… Holy Mary, Mother of God, pray for us sinners now, and at the hour of death… Holy Mary, Mother of God, pray for us sinners now, and at the hour of death…* " Kimmy wasn't particularly religious; this was the only part of the prayer she knew, but at that moment it seemed very fitting even for a dead person. She closed her eyes tightly and prayed.

"They are *evil* Rounds, I told ya. I don't know what her brother ever did to her but she's gonna torture that poor guy for the rest of his life just like my Granny did to me. Nobody should have to live with that and I can stop it."

A thunderous clap reverberated through the night as a transient streak of light raced through Kimmy's clasped and praying hands then exited her back side before the bullet struck Officer Rounds in the chest. Dirk watched as Todd crumpled to the ground. Todd watched as Kimmy's body disintegrated into powder and blew away like ashes on the wind. His blood loss was rapid and he struggled to remain conscious. He struggled to comprehend the event before finally fading into darkness.

"Holy hell, I didn't mean too," Dirk stammered. "I'm sorry Rounds." He lurched quickly to his still idling cargo van and sped away.

PART THREE

3

A single soft light illuminated the room. Flesh to flesh, Alex and Amelia enjoyed the quiet harmony that followed passion. All at once, like rogue lightening, a white light streaked through the room followed by a whoosh of air. It moved quickly through the window, into the room and out through the closed door. The wind blew so fast that it knocked the small lamp onto the floor leaving the room in total darkness.

Perplexed and startled they clung to each other. Afraid she had just sealed her fate she whispered to Alex, "If premarital sex is a sin, is it an even greater sin after death?" She tried to recall the verse in Corinthians that claimed unwed fornication was a sin. "When I was fourteen, I went through the whole confirmation ceremony and I remember Pastor Darge repeating this passage from Corinthians over and over. I think he was on some sort of mission to promote celibacy in our tiny town. I can't remember it word for word but it went something like "fornication is a sin unless every man has his own wife and every woman her own husband." She sat up in bed and wrapped the sheet around her tightly. "Did we just sin in a holy house? Is that what that was, a warning?"

I don't know what that was," he responded, "but I know that scripture. My grandmother and I had a few debates on that one." He hopped spryly from the bed, retrieved the fallen lamp and clicked it on. Standing boldly and unashamed, naked in the soft light, he removed the Holy Bible from the drawer and flipped to Corinthians 7:2 "Nevertheless, to avoid fornication, let every man have his own wife, and every woman have her own husband."" "Here's my part of the argument," he continued. "7-6" " ' But I speak this by permission, and not by commandment.' " "This was Paul's opinion and not God's commandment. I even got my Grandmother to agree. So we're in the clear," he reassured her.

Here was the most perfect man, she thought to herself, naked as the day he was born with the open Bible reading scripture. She had never seen anything so divine. Amelia did feel better. She sighed loudly with both relief and content.

"And just for the record," he continued, "if you would have me, I would make you my wife. She flipped back the covers and exposed her body. "I do," she said.
Alex slid again into the bed beside her.

***

Warm massaging fingers of water worked her naked body to a never before experienced state of relaxation. Amelia filled her lungs with the moist steam as she fully enjoyed the sensation. Not another moment mattered to her but the one she currently enjoyed. Finally and reluctantly she turned off the water and stepped from the tub onto a warm fuzzy bath matt. Water streamed down the mirror in numerous tiny flows when she wiped her hand across its surface to peer. She felt womanly and beautiful and that was the reflection that greeted her.

A firm knock at the door startled her. I must have really lost myself in the moment she thought to herself. I can't believe he's gotten cleaned up that fast. She wrapped the towel around her dripping body and realized it must be Kimmy returning, not wanting to walk in on an intimate moment.

Hair dripping and towel clinging to her damp torso she opened the door with a smile.

"We need to talk." Evron's voice lacked the booming forceful tenor she was used to. His large frame filled the doorway so that she didn't even see Alex until he followed Evron into the room, his curls still disheveled and his khaki brown tee-shirt still wrinkled; his expression equally furrowed.

Amelia's smile had vanished immediately when she saw the big man, replaced rapidly with a quizzical look, which morphed into the features of dread when she saw Alex.

"You should sit down," Evron instructed. His voice almost sounded regretful.

She and Alex sat on the edge of Kimmy's bed, her own bed still tossed from the evening's activity. Alex gently placed his arm around her shoulder and held her close against him. He braced for the news Evron was about to deliver.

I can't believe I'm going to receive my judgment wearing nothing but a towel she thought.

The silence in the room seemed eternal. When finally Ervon spoke he addressed the closed door, not looking at the two sitting near him.

"I have been informed that a short time ago Kimberly Shobek's soul was destroyed." His jaw quivered and his large hands clenched to fight back mixed sorrow and anger.

"No, No, No..." Amelia denied forcefully. "She's coming back, she was only gonna be gone a little while." Her voice broke with tears, "she's….she's coming back." She looked at Alex, her wild eyes pleading for answers, for validation that it couldn't be true but she was only met with sympathy.

"I'm sorry," he said reaching out to hug her. Tears reluctantly streamed down his own cheeks. She pushed away from him and rushed past Evron into the still steaming bathroom where she locked the door turned on the shower and stepped into the warm tub again. Hugging her trembling body, she slid down the tile wall into a fetal position. A stream of tears and water gushed over her.

"I gotta stop him Alex," Evron said flatly. "This place is my job and you kids are more than my job. I'm the Guardian, supposed to keep you all safe. I gotta stop him."

Alex knew the big man was going after him and he tried to reason, "I don't know how you can fight someone like that. He hits you once, you're gone, I mean gone for good. You can't win that fight. You'll just give him one more trophy on his shelf."

"I think I know how…. but I'm gonna need some help. The Harger Blish has only 48 hours left. I'm gonna need to move on this tomorrow night. I promise you won't ever even see the man." His voice begged for Alex's help. "I won't put you in any danger."

"I'm in. Danger or not…he's gotta be stopped."

PART THREE

4

"I knew something had happened last night," she explained to him while she stroked the damp hair away from his feverish brow. "There was this crazy flash of light that hit me last night and knocked me to the ground. I was really upset. I paged you a dozen times." Todd continued to breathe in and breathe out without response. "About twenty minutes later I got the call that you'd been shot." A nurse interrupted her confession when she walked into the room. She checked Todd's vitals and his saline drip then she traded a clean kidney pan for the one that Laurie had been puking in.

***

Jimmy coughed as many chain smokers do; that dry sound of a burning throat that turns wet when exposed to prolonged moisture. On this morning, the unusually hot spring sun boiled the humid air. He waited for the cross walk light to change, a package marked Capital City florist in his hand. At room 5624 he straightened the name plate. Hope's hair had grown back on the side of her head so that it was straight and thick again. Someone; an orderly or nurse most likely, had pinned it back with a pink ribboned bobby pin. Jimmy took the vase with the wilted daisies to the sink. He dropped the daisies in the trash and filled the vase with fresh water and flowers. He placed them by her bedside and went to the window to open the blinds. "Hi Hope, would you like to feel the sun on you face for a while?" He sat in the chair close to the bed. "Your hair looks very pretty today." He sat silent for a while next to the bed organizing his own thoughts. "Listen here little one,… I used to call my sister that – Little One. She said she hated it but she always smiled when I said it." He had gotten off track and redirected himself. "My addiction counselor says that I need to let go of my guilt and move past the grieving stage. He told me I need to *express* my feelings to my friends and family, not to validate them but to release them. If I told this to my friends and family they'd look at me like I was really nuts. So I'm gonna unload on you for a while. Ok?"

225

"I've been pretty screwed up for a long time now. I could blame Mom for getting so fu--," he looked at the little girls innocent faced and rephrased, "*screwed* up on heroin that she practically died from it – well, technically, she died from an infection but it was probably from the needles. I could blame Dad for not caring about us but I think that it was more that he didn't care *for* us. I don't think he knew how to. He drank , *a lot*," he emphasized. "Probably because he missed Mom, probably because he didn't know how to handle two whiny brats."

He sighed heavily before taking on the next family member. "Kimmy was just four years old. She didn't remember much of Mom and she relied a lot on me. I was eleven when Mom died. She'd been in and out of the hospital for months so I was pretty used to taking care of Kimmy and myself by then. I fixed meals, mostly cold cereal and peanut butter sandwiches. Dad would sometimes forget to leave money for groceries. I'd put Kimmy in the wagon and we'd walk up to Hy-Vee. It's not easy to get across Euclid Avenue in just one light when you're pulling a wagon full of pop bottles and a four year-old. We'd cash in the cans and buy milk, bread and candy. I remember one time when Kimmy was sick with a bad cold. We paid for the groceries and on the way home I noticed Kimmy was eating some candy; turns out she swiped a bag of cough drops. She was five and the first thing she ever swiped was cough drops."

"She was a pretty self-sufficient little kid. When I was about fifteen I started resenting the responsibility and spent more time with friends and less time at home. At eight years old Kimmy pretty much had the house to herself. When she started missing school a lot I remember Dad would yell at her. She'd complain about one thing or another hurting – her head, her back, her legs. Dad cussed and threw things. Once, when the school told him that she hadn't been there for a week and that I was calling in sick for her, Dad kicked a hole in the wall and broke his toe." He smiled remembering the scene.

"Turns out she wasn't faking it. MS is just that way; you can't pin point a specific area that hurts because the hurt travels. Dad didn't have good insurance and could rarely pay the doctors. When Kimmy was about ten I came home from a party around three in the morning, she was lying in the hallway between the kitchen and the living room with a blanket around her. She was trembling so hard I could feel the floor shaking. I was too tanked to drive her to the hospital and Dad wasn't home so I called an ambulance. I left a note for dad." He grimaced remembering the scene. "Wow he was mad when he got to the hospital the next morning. He said I was gonna have to sell my car to pay the bill. They diagnosed her with MS a few days later and Dad never mentioned it again. After that he was sober for two weeks. He almost never left the hospital. I'd go to school and come back to the hospital after school. He'd be sitting in the same chair, sometimes still in the same clothes. I even remember him crying. I was kinda glad when he started drinking again; at least that seemed normal."

"Dad explained to the school about Kimmy's MS and her treatments. Things returned to our idea of normal. Kimmy's bad days were less frequent with the drugs, at least for a while. She actually led a pretty normal existence: parties, friends, boys, typical rebel teenager stuff. She hung out with an interesting group of kids, artsy types. The girl could really draw. She was good. I still have her sketches at home."

Jimmy reached for the non-existent pack of smokes in his shirt pocket. Remembering he'd quit, he pulled the cinnamon toothpick from atop his ear and placed it in his clenched teeth. "Then, in her senior year, she started getting sick more often. Dad didn't want to deal with it. I think it was too painful, too much a reminder of Mom's long illness. I sure didn't want to deal with it. I was still running with the same crowd of losers I left high school with. We partied a lot." He remembered the drugs and the booze and said to Hope, "Let's just leave it at that, you're too young to know the rest." "Anyway," he continued, "in the end I wasn't around for her much, neither was Dad, neither were her friends. She spent her last two months in this hospital just two floors up. In that whole time I only came to see her four times and even then it was just for a few minutes."

"She had a roommate that only she could understand. A girl who, I guess, used to be beautiful and athletic until she got into a car

228

accident. She was a quadriplegic; doctors said she was lucky to be alive. I guess she didn't think so. She and my sister both checked themselves out of this place permanently a couple of months ago. "I played the 'if only' game for a long time: if only I'd come to see her more often so she had someone to talk to, if only I had taken more interest in her art work, if only I had bothered to find out more about that fucking disease I could have gotten her to the doctors sooner." Wiping the tears streaming down his face with the sleeve of his shirt, he sniffed then took a long breath.

"When I sobered up a few weeks after the funeral, I kept thinking about you." He smiled through his tears at the little girl. "I'd be driving around the city aimlessly and find myself here. I remember your nurse, Sarah, she's the pretty one," he whispered to Hope. "She said that you never had visitors. I guess I thought that since I didn't visit Kimmy here much that maybe I could help you….," his words trailed off. "Christ!" he said, mad at himself for slipping into denial again. "To be honest, I did this more for my own selfish reasons to make me feel better about failing Kimmy. I don't know if you can hear me. The doctor says no, but if you can I want to say thank you for letting me be here for you. You've helped me through a rough time kiddo and I hope that my voice has made your life a little more bearable too."

Again, Jimmy wiped the tears from his eyes, this time forcefully as he straightened his posture. "Now let me tell you Hope,

I'm gonna make it. I'm not drinking anymore, gave up the smokes too," he leaned in to whisper in her ear "and I've got a date this Friday with your pretty nurse, Sarah."

Standing beside her bed, he addressed her with conviction. "Let me tell you something little one, I got on with my life and it's time you got on with yours too. I let go of the bottle, the guilt and most of the pain." With a whisper he admitted, "I even started reading scriptures. I'm not ready for organized religion, mind you, but I want to believe there's more to life than our physical existence. I wanna believe that song," he sang softly, "May the circle be unbroken, bye and bye, Lord bye and bye, there's a better place a waiting…"

Sarah leaned in the doorway and finished the song – "in the sky, Lord, in the sky." Her cheerful smile and sweet voice warmed his soul. She had agreed to their date only on the condition of sobriety. She didn't know yet that he had thrown out the cigarettes too.

"I know the doctors say she can't hear but she still has a soul. I want her to know she's not alone and that her presence has been meaningful." He looked at the little angel in the bed and told her, "Thank you for being a good listener and thanks for introducing me to this pretty nurse."

Sarah whispered from behind him, "I think she knows."

Remarkably Hope responded; a loud and steady beep filled the room, a flat line spread across her monitor. The pulse oximeter registered no number. Brushing the back of his hand lightly across the little girl's cheek, he was both sad for his loss and happy for her continued journey.

"Amazing," said Sarah.

"Good bye Little One."

PART THREE

5

"Cooper drives a '73 Ford E 200 cargo van. It's white, rusty and, fortunately, common. The preservation society was able to find a match; they put on some tread worn Firestone 85/R16, same as Dirks." Evron, Alex and, Amelia planned the night's activities as they sat in the great empty dining hall.

"You've done your homework," Amelia responded. She was tired but groomed.

"Amelia, I want you to head over to the senior center across from Dirk's house. It's bingo night so there will be plenty of people for cover. Dirk usually leaves for work around 9PM. When you see the van leave, call this number." He handed her a small piece of paper. "Two pergs employed at the Iowa Beef Packers will deliver two meat coolers. Make sure they plug in the working one. The other cooler is gonna smell like hell. It broke down about two weeks ago and they just cleaned out the rotten meat and maggots." He grimaced and curled his nose at the thought of the stench. "That's absolutely a perg job."

He continued, "When they're done they'll deliver you to the old Berwick Cemetery east of Ankeny."

"I thought all of the victims...most of the victims," Alex corrected himself; Kimmy had been cremated, "were from Glenndale."

"Glenndale's crawling with cops, "he explained. "The Berwick Cemetery is in farm country; no street lights and not much used. More importantly, it has a new resident; Ethel Hawthorn was buried two days ago." They all knew the plan from there.

Fresh dirt mounded the site, no marker was in place. The cemetery was a walk-in, vehicles were supposed to park along the road but Evron managed to drive the van along the forested edge of the cemetery narrowly missing bordering gravestones. When Alex opened the door to exit, Evron grabbed his sleeve. "You stay on the grass. I don't want your foot prints in the dirt." Alex looked a bit confused until he saw Evron produce a heavy left boot – two sizes too big. It had a two inch solid buildup on the sole to provide a limping gate.

The cool April night was intermittently shadowed by broken clouds floating across the aged gravestones. A screech owl shrieked sporadically; each time it startled Alex. "Funny thing for a dead man to say, but I get the feeling this place is haunted," he remarked.

It was past 10PM when their shovels struck Ethel's coffin, past 11PM when they lifted her rigored corpse from the casket. Dirt from the hole was neatly dumped onto a large tarp to the far side of the pit. Amelia had arrived a while ago and had spread a green tarp on the near side of the hole. Wasted away with age, Ethel's ninety years had taken most of her body mass so Amelia found it fairly effortless to hoist her from the ground as the guys pushed from below. Suddenly, bright headlights bathed Amelia where she stood holding Ethel's form under the arm pits as a car turned off the highway and continued on NE Berwick Drive, out of sight. It wasn't until that point of the night that she had actually felt frightened. Everyone felt the sense of urgency to complete the task and quickened their pace.

Before closing the casket Evron emptied the contents of a small Ziploc onto the satin pillow; three straight brown hairs. With the dirt remounded and the corpse secure in the van they readied to return to Dirk's house. Carefully Evron maneuvered the van with Alex directing the way from outside. "Back about six inches," Alex quietly instructed. The van's left tire rolled slightly up onto the fresh dirt. Producing a half smoked filterless Lucky Strike, Evron flicked it from the driver's window.

Dirk's delivery shift ran from 10 to 2. He was generally home by 2:30. Just short of 2AM they rolled into his driveway, unloaded Ethel into the working freezer and stowed the shovels behind the broken one.

***

In the great empty dining hall, three Budweiser's waited on ice at a lone candle lit table. Grimy and grinning they toasted their efforts and toasted their lost friends. Alex and Amelia were certain they had saved the Harger Blish; Evron was certain he had more to do but this last part he had to do alone.

"Des Moines Police Department, is this an emergency?" the switchboard operator inquired. Evron placed the call from the senior center pay phone.

"I think someone's been shot, 2501 SE Vale Street. I think it's got something to do with that serial grave robber..... No I ain't giving my name, I don't want to be involved but I just saw him pull what looked like a body out of his van and after that I heard a gunshot." He hung up the phone.

The mid-morning sun warmed the filthy screen door pungent with dust. Once inside, Evron smelled strong coffee and heard the low murmur of Days of Our Lives down the hall. With purpose and valor he proceeded. A toilet flushed and Dirk stepped into the hallway, his index finger rooted around in his ear while he multitasked with the other hand trying to shut off the bathroom light switch that he had misjudged.

"HOLY SHIT!" Terror consumed him as he threw himself against the back wall of the hallway. Lurching with panic he fell into the doorway of his bedroom and scrambled for the 9mm he kept in the night stand. Evron followed calmly. Dirk had wedged himself into the far corner of the small room, the pistol unsteady in his shuddering hands. The entire length of his body convulsed, involuntarily rebelling against the directive to be still. He could barely hold the gun straight and steady enough to fire. With a loud explosion the bullet smashed the mirror three feet to the left of Evron's head.

The only barrier between them, a disheveled double bed; Dirk screamed, "What the fuck do you want?" Distant sirens were closing in.

"I am gonna fuck with you every day of your life. I'm gonna hide in every shadow. I'll be in every dark room, I'll torture you every opportunity I get. You see... your Granny and I made a deal..." Evron boldly tormented. "I'm taking over now, it's my turn to *put you through hell!*" Evron could hear the sirens were very close. He leapt up onto the bed and lunged for Dirk. With another explosion Evron collapsed. The red twirling lights of two police cars created a kaleidoscope effect as they bounced off of the various mirrors giving the small room a twisted fun house ambiance. Completing the effect was the rapidly decomposing corpse of Evron James Brown which spewed onto Dirk's bed sheets. The flesh of his face fell onto Dirk's pillow just as two officers swung into the room with their guns drawn.

***

Detectives Crandall and Hawthorn arrived on the scene as Dirk Cooper was dragged from the house bound and laced into a restraining jacket. His wild eyes screamed inside his bobbling head while his asymmetrical lower extremities, minus a prosthetic, spasmed wildly.

"Gonna be tough for the state to fight the insanity plea on that guy." Tom remarked.

"Ov, ov, over h, h, here," the agitated young officer stuttered, motioning to Laurie and Tom from the side of the house. The warming late morning sun had just begun to reach the antiquated coolers against the south east corner of the house. The second cooler still hummed but the first, with flies buzzing about, was silent. The putrid smell wafted into their nostrils and rested on their salivating taste buds. Laurie lifted the lid. Except for maggots, some black acrid substance on the bottom surface and the revolting odor, it was empty. She dropped the lid and puked. Tom, his nose buried in the crook of his elbow, tried to casually avoid Laurie's vomit as well as other repugnant odors. He opened the second cooler where he discovered Aunt Ethel. He too turned and vomited.

PART THREE

6

"Cooper is a real head case," Laurie explained to Todd, weak but awake. Unconscious for seventy-two hours following surgery to repair lacerations to his left kidney, spleen and liver, Todd was understandably lethargic yet amazingly coherent. He absorbed every detail as she spoke. "He claimed the rotting corpse on his bed tried to kill him so he shot it; and here's a weird coincidence for ya, the body in the freezer was Ethel Hawthorn… Tom's aunt." Todd's eyes widen with surprise. "We investigated the grave site that afternoon, found fresh tire tracks fitting Cooper's van and a Lucky Strike cigarette butt, his brand. But the nail in the coffin 'so to speak' was actually the hair in the casket. DCI called this morning; it's Dirks. I'd say the serial grave robber case is closed."

She reached into the duffel bag by her feet and pulled out a half empty sleeve of saltines. Munching while she talked, "Guy's been locked up in Broadlawn's psych ward since they brought him in; keeps screaming that his Grandmas after him."

"He admitted to shooting you," she added "said he was trying to kill the ghost that was standing between you."

Todd watched the cracker projectiles fly from her lips as she spoke. Feebly, he inquired, "Did they find another body at The Cave that night?" She shook her head no, her mouth too full to reply. "He told me he saw Kimberly Shobek standing between us; the suicide / homicide case from Mercy," he reminded unnecessarily. Todd was about to give her the details of the entire odd event but hesitated; unsure what part of his story was wound induced hysteria. "You might want to search the grave sight of this Shobek girl."

"Can't, she was cremated."

The image of the young woman disintegrating before him became more than imagination. His mind dwelled there for only a moment before Laurie interrupted. She stood, ran to the bathroom and vomited into the toilet.

"You ok?" he asked, his voice finding some strength with concern.

"Yep. Just a little morning sickness."

***

With each step spring grass bent beneath her bare feet while the print behind slowly gave way to the grass's untrodden prior form. Well-worn Puma sneakers dangled from her right hand, a sock in the toe of each. In her other hand was a ticket and a single coin. Blue jeans, a red sweatshirt embossed with the gold letters ISU, her long blond hair pulled through the back of a tan ball cap; Amelia awaited the ferry.

"Do you smell that?" Alex asked.

"You mean the smell of fresh cut grass?"

"No, the bread," he emphasized inhaling deeply.

Finches flitted in and out of fragrant lavender lilac bushes on the hill above the riverbank. In a massive Iowa Oak a mourning dove's gentle rocking rhythm seemed to be lulling the lazy river. Beneath the oak, near a white path which paralleled the waterway, an elderly couple sat holding hands on a park bench; the same couple who had sat silently together in the hotel, the coffee shop and the very bench on the day Amelia first arrived. It wasn't until they heard the creaking of the dock that they realized the ferry had arrived. The modest vessel was merely a wooden floating platform with low backed benches at the perimeter of three sides and a meager railing across the bow. It

241

gently nudged the platform and a lone man in humble linen garb secured the moorings and unclipped the shiny golden rope to allow access to those ticketed passengers awaiting passage. Amelia quickly replaced and laced her sneakers.

"It's our turn," Alex whispered quietly." He knew she felt unworthy. The white envelope simply said Amelia. Inside were two white slips of paper; the first a note which read "Congratulations Amelia, you've earned it. Evron," The other was a one way ticket.

In the great hall the double doors were open as passengers again arrived. Some were returning to the Harger Blish, others arriving for the first time. In the center of the great hall, where once stood a giant fig tree encircled by overstuffed sofas, there stood a bronze sculpture of a big man. The placard read, "For selflessly sacrificing his soul so that we may live, Evron James Brown will not be forgotten."

"This is your ticket Amelia; you wouldn't be standing here if it weren't," Alex reassured. He took her hand; they took a breath and boarded the ferry. Amelia presented the porter with her ticket then pressed a small coin discretely into his palm. For just a moment she searched his eyes, for truth, understanding, guidance or maybe just to say thank you. The words made her feel better. "Thank you," she said.

Ready to begin their new journey together, she snuggled into Alex's embracing arms and waited for the ferry to depart. Birds, a gentle breeze, sun light dimmed and shined by a constant stream of lazy puffy clouds on a brilliant blue sky; it was a perfect setting for this ethereal departure but the ferry didn't move.

A small girl with long raven pig tails bounced into view. A white number five gleamed against the navy cotton jersey of her pristine softball uniform. Her gleeful gate turned into an all-out sprint when the elderly couple on the bench stood. Hope threw her little arms around her grandfather's waist in a hug as hard and happy as only a child can give. Her grandmother bent to her knees and showered the girl with kisses. Without a word, each grandparent took a hand and the three boarded the boat.

***

The quiet room was sterilized in white, a mattress on the floor, a forlorn wooden rocker, a porcelain sink and commode. Crouched atop the mattress in the corner Dirk covered his knees with the gown beneath which he wore no other clothing. Eyes frightfully widened and affixed to the bent old woman with exceptionally long fingernails who dutifully swept his floor. Softly she sang, "we're all crazy, we're all crazy."

"Don't worry Stephen; I'll visit you every day." His grandmother emphasized with a wink and a crooked toothless smile.

RE: GENERATION
Coming Fall 2013

Kimmy crawled up his glimmering chest and hungrily kissed his neck, his ear lobe and his jaw line, finally landing again firmly upon his lips.

"It's nice to find a woman who knows what she wants," JT smiled approvingly at Kimmy from the flat of his back.

"I'd have kissed you in line today if you'd have held me a moment longer," she quipped as she rolled from the bed and strolled confidently to the adjacent bath room. With her naked back to him, he puzzled over the star burst patterned scar that matched the one he had discovered on her abdomen.

Kimmy returned to find that JT had straightened the bedding and replaced the pillows but still lay exposed and wanting. She admired his form before sliding in beside him.

"What's the scar?" he asked tracing the outline on her flat belly while sending toe curling twinges through her body.

"Gun shot." His eyes widened in horror but she didn't let him suffer long. "It's a birthmark," she smiled.

"My turn," she said as she reciprocated the twinges by tracing the outline of his rigid lower abdominal muscles. 'What's the JT stand for?"

He released a deep and somewhat sullen breath. "James the Third. It's actually Evron the Third but ET really didn't work for me."

245

***

While taking the campus bus back to her apartment, two oddly familiar faces sat silently staring. With typical brazen attitude Kimmy confronted, "Do you know me?"

"Yes," replied Alex and Amelia, "…and we need your help."

***

Katherine K. Rounds; (AKA, Kimmy), Amelia, Alex and JT travel the world to stop a Seer. As children, Cason Carter and Kimmy were trapped for three days in Cozumel's hidden Mayan ruins. Cason, now a world famous archeologist, is unearthing hidden burial sites and destroying souls on a global scale. As the group closes in, Alex and Amelia may be among his next victims.